THE TERRIBLE TWO

SUMMER IS DIFFERENT. Summer is strange. Time slows and drifts. Bees hover, suspended over flowers, their bellies brushed gold. School is out. Days are long. The sun lingers in the sky, and when it sets, the sky glows for hours. It's an in-between time. You are no longer in the grade you finished last spring; you are not yet in the grade you will start in the fall. There are no school days, no weekends. Monday is meaningless. One day slides gently into the next. It's hard to keep track.

Days indoors. Days outdoors. Days down in your best friend's basement, searching for the seventh secret coin in the desert world of that one video game. Sprinkler days. Water balloon days. Days memorizing dance routines off the internet. The days trying all forty-three flavors of ice cream at the ice cream parlor, and the days figuring out the perfect combination of flavor and cone (sugar, cake, waffle; plain or chocolate dipped). Swimming days. Days looking up cheat codes for games you already beat. Days your best friend goes on vacation, and you watch TV shows you've already seen because you don't want

to do anything new till your best friend gets back. Days making secret potions with stuff from the pantry. Days your dad makes you go golfing. Days building a waterslide park for ants. Days at the movie theater, in air-conditioning, sucking soda through a licorice straw while things explode on-screen. In the fall, it will be dark and chilly, and you will look back and remember fifty different kinds of day, and it will be like you lived fifty different summers. This book is about a summer in the woods.

AH, SUMMER IN YAWNEE VALLEY! Welcome,

welcome. Smell the wildflowers blooming in the woods! Smell the cows, who bend down with hungry lips to tear those wildflowers from their stems, chewing them, swallowing them, and regurgitating them, up and down, to and fro, from mouth to stomach to mouth again, for hours and hours, till their petals, pistils, and stamens have degraded into cud, which the cows finally digest. Sorry! That was disgusting. But hey, the

flowers have nice names! Peaseblossom and thistle, broom and leek. Cowslips, hawthorn, eglantine. And, of course, heartsease, known too as Johnny-jump-up, or love-in-idleness, or the field violet.

If you've read the first two books in this series, *The Terrible Two* and *The Terrible Two Get Worse*, you know the field violet is a special kind of flower. The field violet is the *state* flower. And if you know that, then you probably know it's illegal to pick them. It's not like you'd get sent to jail. Still, it's frowned upon. You could get in trouble.

Of course, trouble never stopped these two, and it probably never will.

That's a lot of violets!

"One of us smells like a turkey," said Miles. (He's the one on the right.)

"What?" said Niles. (He's the other one, the one on the left.)

"Like a turkey," said Miles. "Like Thanksgiving dinner. One of us smells like Thanksgiving dinner."

"Oh," said Niles. "Yeah. That's you."

"What?" said Miles. "How do you know it's me?"

Niles pointed to a couple of places on Miles's outfit. "You're wearing sage. And leeks. You rub that stuff on a turkey."

"You could have warned me!" said Miles.

"I said just do violets."

It's true. Niles had said that. But early that morning, when they were scrounging flowers in the forest for camouflage, Miles had thought it'd be cool to have some variety. A little white. A couple shades of purple. So he'd picked some leeks and some sage and even some wild garlic. Now that he was belly down in a violet patch, breathing hard and baking in the midday sun, Miles was having regrets.

When Miles had regrets, he tended to act as if he had no regrets.

"Well, I still think it looks good," said Miles.

"I even think it smells good," said Niles. "I like turkey."

"Then what the heck are we arguing about?"

"I didn't think we *were* arguing."

"You said I smelled like a turkey!"

"*You* said you smelled like a turkey," said Niles. "I never said anything!"

"How can you say that, when you're saying something right now!"

They continued to argue about whether they were arguing.

Nearby, a branch broke.

A boy cursed. Another boy laughed.

Miles and Niles both shut their mouths.

They buried their heads in the flowers so they blended in with the field, which was on a little hill that overlooked a circle of trees. Miles and Niles crawled forward and took up a post behind a big piece of granite. From there, they could spy on the grove.

There was trash in the grove—crushed cans and magazines torn in half, a crumpled sweatshirt sinking into a mud puddle. An old knife stuck out from a stump. Crudely painted signs were nailed into tree trunks.

The voices in the woods grew louder. Someone delivered the punch line to a bad joke. A rude song was sung badly. And

then three boys burst into the clearing, cackling, shoving, and kicking.

Papa Company.

Two of the boys were hard to tell apart. They wore identical olive drab pants and identical olive drab T-shirts, with little identical olive side caps smashed onto their identical heads. (They were identical twins.)

Miles and Niles kept their eyes on the third boy: the tallest boy, the biggest boy, the boy who was swinging a rusty cage with his left arm.

This boy wore a bunch of heavy military medals pinned to his T-shirt. The decorations pulled his collar down from his

neck and made the whole shirt sag. He looked ridiculous, but the rest of Papa Company (all two of them) didn't think so. His medals demanded respect. They were symbols of power. (They had been purchased, five for three bucks, at a thrift store in downtown Yawnee Valley.)

The leader of Papa Company hung the cage from a low branch at the edge of the clearing. It rattled and shook.

The cage had something inside it.

The thing inside it shrieked.

Up at the rock, Miles craned his head forward and squinted. He wanted to see what was in the cage.

A dark shape flitted around and banged against the metal. The members of Papa Company gathered around and laughed. One poked a stick through the bars. There was more shrieking, some chattering, and a few frantic clicks.

Niles put a hand on his friend's shoulder. "What is it?"

"I think," whispered Miles, "I think it's a squirrel."

"Dumb squirrel," said a boy, down in the grove.

"Yep, it's a squirrel," said Miles.

The leader of Papa Company got bored with the squirrel. He crossed the clearing, pulled the knife from the stump, then plunged it back into the stump.

This was some kind of signal.

The other two boys got quiet.

The leader pointed to one of them.

"Raise the flag, Dugout."

"Yes, sir, Major Barkin, sir," said Dugout, whose real name was Daniel.

"Good," said Major Barkin, whose real name was Josh Barkin. (If you've read the first two books in this series, you probably already figured that out.)

Dugout removed a folded flag from his backpack. Papa Company watched solemnly as he climbed a big oak tree, unfurled the flag, and draped it over a big bough.

The flag showed the white skeleton of a rattlesnake on an all-black field.

Up in his hiding place among the violets, Miles grinned at Niles and raised two fingers in the air.

Niles grinned back and touched his fingertips to his friend's.

Now. If you've read the first two books in the series, you know what's going to happen next. And if you haven't, here's the deal: Josh Barkin and his crew are about to get pranked.

"ROLL CALL!" said Josh.

"DUGOUT!"

"Sir!"

"MUDFLAP!"

"Sir!"

(Mudflap's real name was Tommy.)

This was Papa Company.

The members of Papa Company were cadets at Yawnee Valley Yelling and Push-Ups Camp, a "boot camp for troubled tweens" that operated in these same woods, just a few klicks away.

(At Yawnee Valley Yelling and Push-Ups Camp, distance was measured in klicks. One klick equals .62 miles, which equals 1,091 yards, which equals about 7,900 imperial teaspoons laid end-to-end.)

Josh had been sent to Yawnee Valley Yelling and Push-Ups Camp last year as a punishment. After four weeks at camp, most kids "reformed." They wrote letters begging to come home, promising to be good. But Josh Barkin wasn't like most kids. (He was much worse.) After four weeks, he had asked his parents if he could stay at camp for the rest of the summer. This year he was back. As the only camper in its history to willingly return, Josh was made a JUNECOW, or junior counselor, and given a special hat.

Yawnee Valley Yelling and Push-Ups Camp was an awful place, noisy and violent. But it was Josh Barkin's firmly held belief that even the most awful circumstances could be improved upon—that is, made noisier and more violent—and so he'd recruited two lackeys and given them cool military nicknames in exchange for their total and unquestioning loyalty. This is how Josh became the commander of Papa Company, a renegade cell within the camp. Papa was for the letter *P*—"Papa" is one of the twenty-six code words for the twenty-six letters in the International Radiotelephony Spelling Alphabet. (It starts with Alpha, Bravo, Charlie, and goes through Papa all the way to Zero.) And the *P* also stood for Power, which is what Papa Company was all about. "Papa Company" had a nice military ring to it, plus Power Company sounded like an electric utility.

Almost daily, Papa Company snuck off to the grove, where Josh offered the twins what he called "the real training." Today, as usual, the training topic was "advanced weaponry."

Josh spit out some gum he'd been chewing, because its flavor was all gone.

"Sir, do you want me to pick up that gum and pack it out for you, sir?" asked Mudflap.

"Naw, leave it for the bugs and raccoons to chew on," said Josh.

"Oh, OK, right, makes sense, yes, sir," said Mudflap.

Josh looked at his gum in the dirt. He imagined a beetle rolling the gum all the way back to his home, probably up a big hill, and then stuffing it down through the little hole he used as a front door. His whole beetle family would gather around the wad, so excited, and they'd each break off a little bit with their pincers and chew it. And it wouldn't have any flavor. Heh. Dumb beetles.

Josh smiled.

Then he got serious.

"TEN-HUT, NIMBUSES!"

Ten-hut means "attention." Nobody really knows what nimbus means.

The boys stood straight.

"At EASE, nimbuses."

They both relaxed a little.

"Now . . ." Josh rubbed his chin. "TEN-HUT AGAIN!"

The boys snapped straight.

Josh loved watching the two trembling cadets do whatever he said. When it came to shouting commands, Josh was a master. For proof, you just had to look at "The Yawnee Valley Yelling and Push-Ups Camp Counselor Training Manual," which Josh proudly called "the only book he'd ever finished," and which wasn't a book but was actually a three-ring binder. (He also hadn't finished it.) The manual had a section called "YELLING!" that identified the characteristics of good command voice: PLOP. That was the acronym. (They were big on acronyms at camp.)

The first *P* was for POWER (again) (of course). Josh had been born powerful. Power ran in his family: His father was a school principal, and so was his grandfather, and his great-grandfather, and his great-great-grandfather, and his great-great-great-grandfather. His great-great-great-great-grandfather had been a fur trapper, but you better believe he had been a *powerful* fur trapper. One day, Josh would fulfill his destiny and would himself become a school principal. Or maybe something even more powerful, like a district

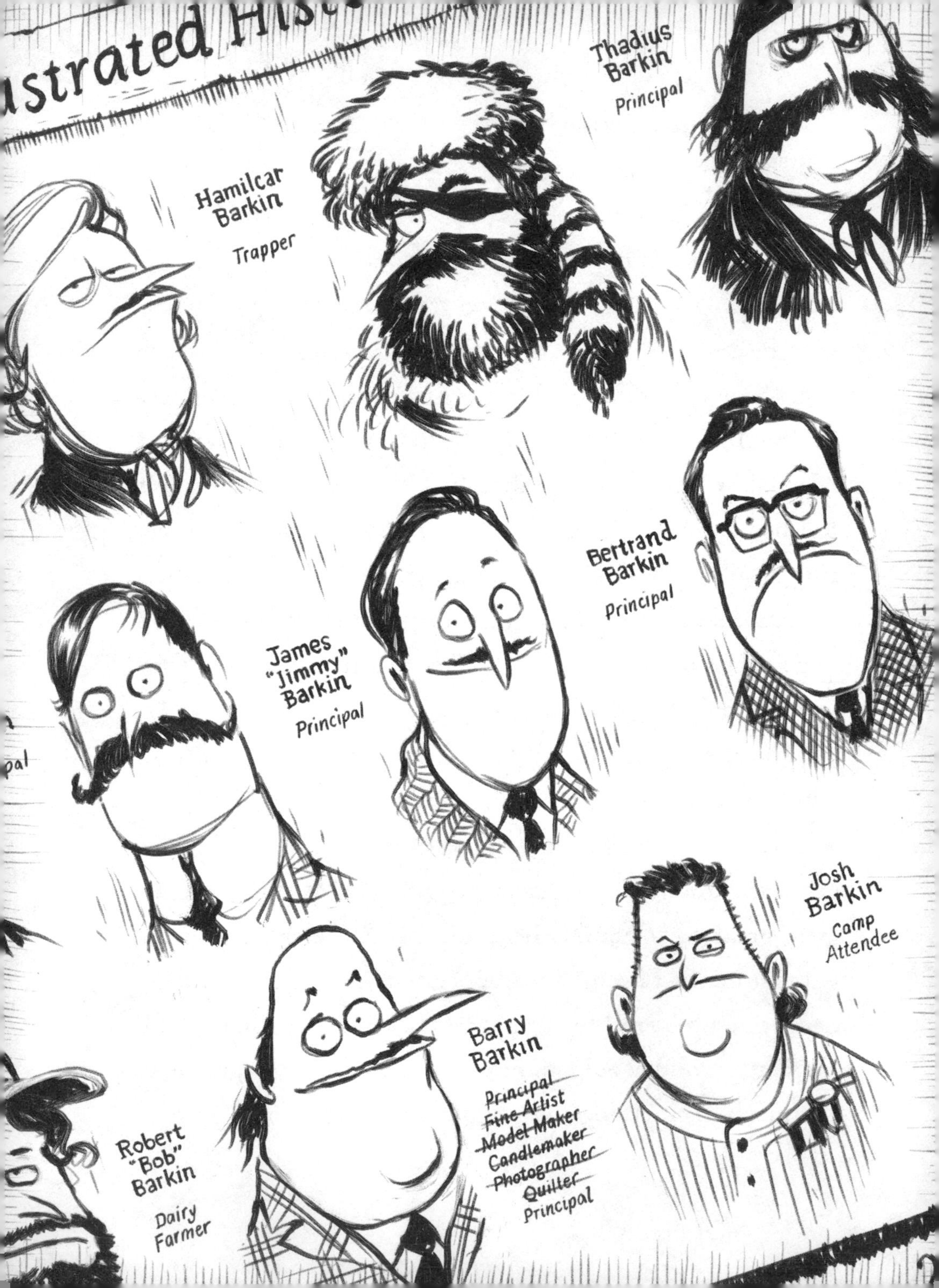

...strated Hist...
Thadius Barkin
Principal
Hamilcar Barkin
Trapper
Bertrand Barkin
Principal
James "Jimmy" Barkin
Principal
...pal
Josh Barkin
Camp Attendee
Barry Barkin
~~Principal~~
~~Fine Artist~~
~~Model Maker~~
~~Candlemaker~~
~~Photographer~~
~~Quilter~~
Principal
Robert "Bob" Barkin
Dairy Farmer

administrator. According to his grandfather, Josh had the hands of a superintendent. "You remind me of me," his grandfather told him. "You are strong. You have authority. You are powerful. Remarkable what skips a generation." So yeah, Josh had the first *P* covered.

The *L* was for LOUDNESS. And Josh was loud. He had "the Barkin Bark," as his mom was fond of saying. She was also fond of saying, "Please quiet down, Josh, I'm trying to watch the news."

The *O* was for the *O* in LOUDNESS, because otherwise the acronym would be PLP, and that's dumb.

And the second *P*? The second *P* was for PROJECTION. It wasn't enough to be powerful and loud. You had to be powerful and loud right into people's faces.

"ABOUT-FACE!" Josh **powerfully**, **loudly** **projected**.

The boys both turned their backs on their leader.

Yes, there was no doubt about it: Josh was a natural PLOPper. He imagined his father watching this drill and smiling proudly. Then he imagined his grandfather's face superimposed on his father's face, because he was mad at his father, and had been for over a year. That wasn't quite right either, so he imagined himself watching himself, and he liked that image quite a bit.

"Right FACE!"

The cadets turned right.

"Left FACE!"

They turned left.

"Right FACE right FACE right FACE left FACE ABOUT-FACE ABOUT-FACE."

The cadets spun around. "Good. That's real good," said Josh. "HAND SALUTE!"

They saluted.

"STOP saluting!"

They didn't stop saluting.

"STOP SALUTING!"

They still didn't stop.

"STOP it, YOU DUMB NIMBUSES!"

The cadets were a little nervous, but they kept their hands to their foreheads.

Josh began to turn a bit purple.

An awkward mike passed.

(At Yawnee Valley Yelling and Push-Ups Camp, time was measured in mikes. A mike is a minute.)

Finally, a cadet spoke up.

"Um? Sir?"

"What is it, Dugout?"

"Sir, that's, well, sir, that's not the command to stop saluting, sir."

"I KNOW THAT IT'S NOT, NIMBUS."

"Sir, of course, sir."

"DUGOUT, GO STAND AND FACE THAT TREE."

"Which tree, sir?"

"That one."

"Yes, sir."

"CLOSER, DUGOUT, LIKE YOU'RE GOING TO KISS THE TREE."

Dugout pressed his nose against the bark.

"HEH!" said their leader. (He actually said "HEH!") "Looks like you're in love with that tree, Dugout."

Mudflap snickered.

"He better watch out for splinters in his lips," said Mudflap.

"That's a great joke, Mudflap!" said Josh.

(It was not a great joke.)

"Hey, Dugout!" Josh said. "That's your new name! Splinters!"

"But I like Dugout," said Splinters, who was hard to understand because he said it directly into a tree.

"Sorry, Splinters."

It was important to cover up any sign of weakness, like forgetting the proper command to stop saluting, and to quash any seeds of insubordination, like some other kid remembering the proper command to stop saluting. Otherwise you could have a mutiny on your hands.

"Forget about that dumb saluting command. That's an order. At ease, nimbuses."

Mudflap stopped saluting. Splinters left his tree.

"Not you, Splinters. You stay over by that tree."

Splinters went back to his tree.

Josh picked up a twisted stick from the ground. "Today's weapon: the throwing stick."

An impressed murmur passed through Papa Company.

"You can do a lot with sticks. Sticks are great weapons. You can poke people with them. You can thump people with them. You can use one as a sword—"

Mudflap lit up at this. He liked swords.

"—but that's for dorks."

Mudflap pretended he had never lit up and didn't like swords.

"But the best thing to do with a stick is to throw it. You can disable an enemy by throwing a stick right at his head."

"Nice," said Splinters.

"*Super* nice," said Mudflap.

"But the most important thing when it comes to throwing sticks is *accuracy*. I'm a really accurate thrower. It's. All. In. The. Arm."

Josh pointed to his arm. Mudflap nodded.

"Allow me to demonstrate," said Josh. "Splinters, turn around."

Splinters faced Josh.

"Sir, are you going to hit me in the head with that stick?" he asked.

"No, don't be a nimbus," said Josh. "What I'm going to do is *not* hit you in the head."

"Oh," said Splinters. "Phew. That's a lot better."

"Accuracy," said Josh.

Mudflap nodded some more.

"Splinters, pick up that rock and balance it on your head. I'm going to hit it off with this stick."

"Sir, why don't you just throw the stick at the rock there, on the ground, and hit it?" Splinters asked.

"*Drama*, Splinters. It's like that guy who shot an arrow through an apple on some nimbus's head," said Josh. "Do you think anyone would remember that guy's name if he'd just shot an apple on a table?"

"Wait, who?"

"You know who I mean," said Josh. "Now put that rock on your head."

Splinters did as he was told.

"Now hold really still." Josh aimed his stick. "Actually, come a little closer."

Splinters took two nervous steps toward Josh.

"Closer."

Splinters took two more.

"Now," said Josh, "watch my arm. Splinters, don't flinch."

"One," said Josh.

"Two," said Josh.

Then Josh threw the stick and hit Splinters in the face.

"Ow!" said Splinters. He was afraid of doing something wrong, so, despite the pain, he remained perfectly still, and the rock remained on his head.

"You missed the rock, sir," said Mudflap, then immediately regretted saying it.

"Of course I did," said Josh. "Why would I hit a dumb rock? I was demonstrating how to hit an enemy in the face."

Mudflap nodded. Splinters didn't, because he had a rock on his head.

"But you said you wouldn't hit me," said Splinters.

"I know I did," said Josh. "I pranked you! It was a prank!"

(It was not a prank.)

Mudflap nodded. "You're a really great prankster, Major Barkin!"

Josh beamed. "Right you are, Mudflap. I'm probably the best."

Over in a field on a nearby hill, it sounded like a rock scoffed.

Josh Barkin held a finger in the air and said, "HUMMUS!" HUMMUS was a military acronym Josh had made up, which in Papa Company meant "Hush Up, My Men, Utter Silence!" and more generally refers to a delicious paste made from garbanzo beans.

"Hummus?" asked Mudflap.

"It means be quiet," said Splinters. "It's another one of those acronyms, from when you had chicken pox."

"Oh!" said Mudflap. "I was thinking of garbanzo beans."

"Yeah," said Splinters, "to be honest, I am too, and I *know* what HUMMUS is supposed to mean."

"Mom makes good hummus," said Mudflap, who suddenly missed home.

"SHUT UP!" said Josh.

Josh wished he was holding another stick so he could throw it at Mudflap's head.

"UTTER SILENCE. Did anybody else hear that rock scoff?"

The cadets turned and stared at the hill for five utterly silent mikes, alert to any sign of trespassers.

Nothing happened.

Josh got bored.

"Eh," said Josh, "it was probably the wind blowing through the violets, or some dumb animal coughing."

Nods all around.

"OK," said Josh, "who's hungry?"

"Me, sir!" shouted the twins, who'd been thinking of hummus for the last six and a half mikes.

"Mudflap, go get the fruit cocktail."

Mudflap crossed the grove and reached into the hollow of a tree, which is where Papa Company stored their snacks. He returned with a can of fruit cocktail so big he had to carry it with both arms. Splinters watched hungrily as Mudflap proudly produced his Swiss Army knife, which combined a number of useless tools into one: a can opener that didn't work, a toothpick that was too thick to get between your teeth and was made of gross plastic, tweezers too dull to pull out a sliver, blunt scissors, and a knife you stabbed yourself with every time you tried to fold it back up. Selecting the can opener, Mudflap began puncturing the lid of the can. Plink, plink, plink. He poked holes along its circumference, working slowly. He sweated a little. Mudflap's right arm got tired, so he switched to his left arm, which got tired even faster. Plink, plink, plink. There was a lot of grunting. His brother's eager eyes made Mudflap nervous, which made the whole thing take longer. Plink, plink.

Three mikes passed and Mudflap was barely more than a quarter of the way around the lid. Three mikes might not seem like a very long time to wait, but put this book down and go stare at a can for 180 seconds. You'll see why Splinters was getting antsy. Splinters stared, starving, marking Mudflap's slow progress with greedy anticipation. He looked lovingly at the label, its drawings of cherries, grapes, pineapples, and pears. And a peach! He read over and over the three most beautiful words in the English language: IN LIGHT SYRUP. It was poetry, that fruit cocktail label, and Splinters imagined the syrup sticking sweetly to his tongue, his lips, his fingertips. (Splinters had a Swiss Army knife too, an identical one, with a spork that couldn't hold food. And so Papa Company ate with their hands.)

Josh, who hated when his cadets' attention was on anything besides him, began to grow jealous of the can. He needed his men's eyes, their minds, their hearts. Papa Company was made in his image, and he hated any indication that these boys were anything else but extensions of his will in the world. The fruit cocktail was a threat to his power. Josh had to do something to reestablish his primacy in the grove.

"Knock, knock," said Josh, sweetly.

Nobody asked, "Who's there?"

"Nimbus," said Josh, sweetly.

Nobody asked, "Nimbus who?"

"Aw, come on, Mudflap. How long are you gonna be with that can?"

"I'm trying," said Mudflap.

And Splinters watched him try.

"OK." Enough was enough. Josh pulled his knife from the stump. "Splinters, bring me that squirrel."

Splinters saw Josh's knife.

Josh had his attention.

"The squirrel, sir?" said Splinters.

"You heard me. The dumb squirrel! Fetch it. Now. That's an order."

Splinters, who hoped Josh did not notice that he had taken the rock off his head and set it quietly on the ground next to him, was eager to earn back his commander's favor. He took the cage down from its branch and set it before Josh's feet.

The squirrel, which had been squeaking this whole time, even during the five mikes of HUMMUS, now began to screech. The sound was almost human.

Josh picked up the cage with his left hand. The knife was still in his right. He stared at the animal behind the wire and laughed.

"Dumb squirrel," said Josh.

Splinters's eyes were on Josh Barkin. Mudflap's eyes were also on Josh Barkin, but his hands were still on the can. He would not be swayed from his task. Josh watched him with contempt. He decided that Mudflap, not Splinters, was definitely his less favorite twin.

"Watch this," Josh said.

Josh raised the knife over his head. The sun shone on the blade, but it was too rusty to gleam. The squirrel was quiet. The cadets were quiet. Even the birds seemed to have stopped their song.

And then Mudflap screamed.

"AHHHHHHHHHHHHHHHHHHHHHHHHHH-HHHHHHHHHHHHHHHHHH!" screamed Mudflap.

The knife hovered in Josh's hand.

Splinters and Josh looked at Mudflap. He'd finally gotten the lid off, and now he was looking into the can and screaming.

"AHHHHHHHHHHHHHHHHHHHHHHHH-
HHHHHHHHHHHHHHHHHHHHHH!"

The can trembled in Mudflap's hands. Splinters ran over and looked inside.

"AHHHHHHHHHHHHHHHHHHHHHHHH-
HHHHHHHHHHHHHHHHHHHHHH!"

Splinters was screaming too now.

A black-and-yellow snake slithered out from the can and wound around Mudflap's hand.

"AHHHHHHHHHHHHHHHHHHHHHHHH-
HHHHHHHHHHH!" continued Mudflap. He threw down the can. Two more snakes fell out and writhed on the forest floor.

"AHHHHHHHHHHHHHHHHHHHHHHHH-
HHHHHHHHHH!" screamed everybody.

Mudflap shook the snake off his hand. It landed on Josh's foot. He dropped his knife and the cage, and wondered what he should do.

"Stay still, sir!" cried Mudflap.

"Kick it off!" cried Splinters. "Move!"

"Nimbuses!" cried Josh.

The snake slid off Josh's foot—and onto his other foot. Then it slithered off that foot too.

Josh thought he might throw up.

Splinters was crying.

Everyone was running around.

"Are they poisonous?" asked Mudflap.

"One bit me," said Splinters, who had not been bitten.

"Smash them!" Josh ordered.

But there was no way anyone was going near those snakes.

Splinters had torn off his shirt and was sucking on his forearm to get the venom out, but there was no venom, because, again, he had not been bitten.

"They're rattlesnakes!" said Mudflap.

"But they don't have rattles!" said Splinters.

"They could be babies," said Mudflap. "Babies' venom is even more deadly than adults'! They haven't learned to control their bites! They just shoot the poison into you!"

Splinters moaned.

And then the rattling began. It was a loud and angry rattling that came from who knows where. In their panic, there was no way the boys could identify the dreaded noise's origins. The rattling seemed to echo through the trees and surround them. (Though if they'd been a little more levelheaded, they might have determined that the sound was coming from the rock in the field on the hill nearby.)

"IT'S THEIR MOM!" screamed Mudflap. "SHE'S GONNA KILL US."

"RUN!" PLOPped Josh. "THAT'S AN ORDER! RUN FOR YOUR LIVES!"

And since they did not know where the rattling was coming from, the three members of Papa Company scattered in three different directions, leaving three harmless garter snakes to happily hunt beetles in the grove.

(Now *that's* a prank.)

UP IN THEIR HIDING PLACE, Miles and Niles set down their baby rattles and laughed. They rested their heads against rocks and laughed the laughs of pranksters, pure-souled laughter that started deep in their bellies and floated high over the breeze. They wiped tears from their eyes, then laughed so hard they cried some more. They were weak from laughing.

Pre-prank, Miles and Niles had outlined a thorough post-prank procedure. It was a two-step plan:

1.   Laugh.
2.   Run away.

Having completed step 1, Miles and Niles should have already been fleeing. But they turned back toward the grove.

"The squirrel," said Miles. "We gotta save it."

"I know," said Niles.

And they slid down the hillside and crept through the trees.

The cries of Papa Company could still be heard in the woods. When the two boys arrived in the clearing, Niles picked up the can of fruit cocktail and admired their handiwork.

Earlier that day, pre-prank, just after dawn, they had scavenged for the perfect sticks—sturdy, straight, and forked at the end—and gone to a pond deep in the woods, where they'd spent the morning looking for snake dens. Miles caught two snakes, Niles one. They carried their quarry in a pillowcase, which writhed as if alive, and stole into the grove, which they'd been watching for weeks. Miles held the pillowcase while Niles had gone to the hollow where Papa Company stored their snacks. He'd opened the can of fruit cocktail from the bottom (with a real can opener, from his kitchen). They'd dumped out the fruit and put in the snakes, and some grass, and some rocks to get the weight right. Niles had poked airholes in the bottom of the can and reattached it, discreetly, with duct tape. (It is a fact of life that nobody looks at the bottom of a can.) At the last second, Miles had added some stinkbugs, as a masterstroke.

Now, back in the clearing, post-prank, Niles sniffed the can and shook his head.

Miles approached and peered over Niles's shoulder. "What happened to the stinkbugs?" he asked.

"I think the snakes ate them," said Niles.

"Dang."

Niles shrugged. "Nature."

Niles put the can in his pack—it would make a good exhibit in the museum Niles was planning, dedicated to their pranking exploits—and the boys cautiously approached the cage.

The squirrel saw them coming and went wild. The cage, which had toppled onto its side, rocked on the forest floor as the animal clattered inside it. The squirrel reared up on its back feet and glared at the boys, chattering.

The boys looked at each other, then back at the squirrel.

Rock paper scissors. They pounded their fists in their palms. Niles shot paper. Miles shot scissors. Niles slapped his flat palm against his forehead. Miles looked relieved.

OK.

Niles inhaled. He slowly reached toward the cage's door.

The squirrel lunged. Niles jumped back.

"Hey," said Niles. "You better do it."

"What?" said Miles. "You lost!"

"Yeah, but you have better reflexes."

Miles considered this. He smiled. Niles had a point. He rolled the sleeves of his T-shirt up to his shoulders.

"Well," said Miles, "if I get rabies, tell my mother I love her."

"If you get rabies, I think you just have to get a bunch of shots. Like twenty. In your stomach."

"Oh," said Miles. "Great."

"Anyway it takes a couple weeks to die of rabies, so you could just tell her yourself."

"Do you want me to do this or not?"

"Sorry."

Miles extended a trembling hand. The squirrel leapt at it, then bounced back from the bars of its cage. Miles flinched, but pressed on. The squirrel was furious and frightened. It leapt and nipped at the air. With an outstretched finger, Miles flicked the latch on the cage and flung the door open.

"HA HA!" Miles said (he actually said "HA HA!") as he rolled away from the cage.

"He's not leaving," said Niles, who had removed himself to a safe spot across the grove, behind a rock.

Niles was right. The squirrel stayed in its cage, staring curiously at the open door.

"Come on, little guy," said Miles. But the squirrel didn't move.

"Hmm," said Miles. "Well, take your time, but we gotta go."

"Hold on," said Niles, popping up from behind his rock.

"What are you doing?" Miles asked.

Niles ran over to the oak, scrambled up into its branches, and inched out onto the bough that held Papa Company's flag.

"Oh," said Miles. "Oh boy." He tried to exchange a conspiratorial glance with the squirrel, which was still in its cage and now appeared to be asleep.

Sitting up on the bough, Niles plucked up the flag and placed it in his lap, where he folded it into a triangle. "Catch!"

Niles tossed the flag to Miles, who tossed it in his pack. They grinned at each other. Niles wrapped his legs around the branch and hung from it upside down. He reached two fingers down, and Miles reached two fingers up, and they exchanged their secret handshake.

"Masterstroke," said Miles.

CLANG!

Over in its cage, the squirrel shrieked and sprung through the door. The boys snapped their heads toward the sound and watched the animal flee

into the woods, which is why they didn't see what scared it off.

Realizing he'd get yelled at, and have to do extra push-ups, if he returned to camp bare-chested, Splinters had come back for his shirt. The cadet now stood on the edge of the clearing, watching Miles and Niles.

"UM THERE ARE TWO GUYS STEALING OUR

FLAG AND THEY'RE DRESSED LIKE GIANT PLANTS!" he shouted.

Then Splinters raised his hands to his mouth and made a series of unpleasant screeches, growls, and hisses. This was the call of the turkey vulture, which was a signal to his squad that their base was under attack.

His call was answered by more screeches, growls, and hisses, and one call of "STOP THOSE NIMBUSES!" The members of Papa Company stormed back through the woods to defend their headquarters.

Niles dropped from the branch and hit the ground hard. Splinters jumped into the clearing and pinned Niles to the ground. Niles struggled, but Splinters pushed his face into the dirt.

"Mrmf," said Niles.

Then Miles charged into Splinters and tore him off his friend.

"Come on!" cried Miles, and bolted toward the woods.

Niles picked himself up and ran after Miles, who was running after the squirrel.

Josh and Mudflap arrived at the grove and saw Splinters on the ground. Josh was embarrassed for the boy, who was definitely now his least favorite cadet. He picked Splinters's shirt off the ground and held it out to him.

"Wait," Josh said. "This is my shirt."

"What?" Splinters asked.

"It says my name on it. All my stuff has my name on it."

Josh pointed to where FUTURE PRINCIPAL JOSH BARKIN was written on the inside collar in big block letters.

"YOU STOLE MY SHIRT!"

"It was a mix-up!"

It had not been a mix-up. Splinters had been wearing Josh Barkin's shirt because he wanted to be like Josh Barkin. Heck, he wanted to *be* Josh Barkin. And if he'd told Josh that, Josh would have been flattered. But instead, Splinters, lying shirtless on the ground, said, "You know how things get mixed up in the barracks!"

"Of course I *know*," said Josh. "That's why my dad wrote my name on all my stuff, nimbus!"

To be honest, Josh wished his dad hadn't written FUTURE PRINCIPAL JOSH BARKIN on all of his clothes. He'd been having second thoughts about his future. In fact, Josh had decided that he didn't want to be a principal like his father. He wanted to be

a principal like his *grandfather*. And so he wished his grand-father had written FUTURE PRINCIPAL JOSH BARKIN on all of his clothes.

"Sir?" said Splinters, who was wondering why Josh was gazing forlornly at the stump. Josh shook his head.

Splinters looked down.

"A hundred push-ups when we get back to camp. Plus however many push-ups the supreme commander gives you for showing up out of uniform."

Splinters sniffed. "Yes, sir."

"Which way did they go?" Josh asked.

Splinters pointed.

"Follow me, nimbuses!" Josh cried out. "Let's get those nimbuses!"

He crashed into the forest, waving the shirt above his head.

Mudflap considered helping his brother up, but he turned and followed Josh instead.

JOSH PURSUED MILES AND NILES through the woods. He employed the wilderness tracking skills he'd learned at Yawnee Valley Yelling and Push-Ups Camp: searching for snapped twigs, examining bent blades of grass, but mainly following two pretty clear sets of bootprints in the mud.

Over log and through bush, Josh stomped after his prey, all the while making disgusting vulture sounds as a signal for his cadets to follow. He gurgled triumphantly. He hacked rowdily. They were on the enemy's trail.

Ah! The thrill of the chase! Was there anything better? Maybe the next part, the thrill of the catch. And the part after that, the thrill of the beatdown. When Josh really thought about it, it was all pretty good. And thrilling!

Josh spied a green-and-purple clump just off the trail. He kneeled and picked up a pair of suits made from flowers.

Camouflage. Very clever. Josh knew of only two dumb nimbuses smart enough to come up with something like this.

"What is it, sir?"

Mudflap had caught up with his leader and was standing at a respectful distance.

"Couple of ghillie suits," Josh said. "They probably ditched them so they could run faster."

Mudflap nodded, impressed.

But was he *sufficiently* impressed? The cadet's face held something other than the expression of unalloyed admiration Josh expected from his charges. Was it doubt? Did Mudflap doubt his tracking abilities? Was that what was in his face? Doubt? Or insolence? Or doubt *and* insolence?

(In fact, Mudflap was just afraid of getting hit in the head with a stick, like his brother.)

Josh pressed his nose into the damp suits and inhaled deeply. "They're close. Very close," he said, then coughed violently because he had some garlic in his nose.

The forest filled with answering coughs.

"That wasn't a turkey vulture cough, Splinters!" Mudflap called to his brother, trying to be helpful. "Major Barkin is actually just on the ground coughing! I think he got something in his nose!"

What was this nimbus thinking? Josh leapt to his feet. There was purple rage in his face and a brown stick in his hand.

"What did you tell your brother that for, Mudflap?"

"Sorry, sir."

"What is this, a mutiny? Are you a mutineer, Mudflap?"

"No, sir."

Josh raised his stick.

"Step closer, Mudflap. Get in stick range."

"Sir?"

But Mudflap was saved by news from Splinters. "I see them!"

Josh let out a joyous bellow. He dropped the stick and resumed the hunt.

"Over here!"

"They're running!"

"There! There!"

Josh ran. He tore through the trees.

Mudflap stood on a tree stump and pointed due north.

"That way! That way!"

Josh ran.

There! Ahead. Maybe fifty yards away. Two boys. They appeared in flashes, between the trees. Josh recognized them immediately. Miles Murphy. Niles Sparks. The banes of the Barkins. Nimbuses. Nemeses.

Now this was personal.

Of course, it had gotten personal as soon as they'd stolen that flag, which Josh had designed himself. The rattlesnake skeleton being a symbol of him *personally*—Josh was fierce, like a rattlesnake, and really cool, like a skeleton—as well as a symbol of Papa Company. And of course Papa Company was also personal, since really what was Papa Company but an extension of Josh's person, specifically the fist part of his person, a figurative fist that was now on its way to punching those two jokers in their literal heads.

Anyway, now it was really, really personal.

Josh ran.

The blond one, Niles, was getting tired. He never had been much of an athlete. And as long as Miles kept waiting up for his little friend, Josh would be able to catch them both. Thirty-five yards. Josh grinned. He ran.

Josh couldn't believe his luck! These nimbuses were headed straight for the meadow. A great wide meadow by a mossy pond, with a few dumb trees and nowhere to hide. They'd be easily spotted, easily caught, easily thrashed. Yes! Josh would thrash those two nimbuses and then throw them in the pond! But he had to remember to get his flag back before the pond part, or else the flag would get all wet.

"To the meadow!" Josh cried.

Josh glimpsed them again—no more than twenty yards ahead. He splashed through a creek. Close now. Almost to the meadow. Branches whipped his arms. Thorns pierced his calves where his camp socks had fallen down. But Josh felt no pain. He ran. He ran.

The woods thinned and then stopped, and Josh charged into the meadow. A bevy of quail startled and beat a low path toward the pond.

"What the glug?" said Josh.

The meadow was empty.

He got down on his hands and knees to study the ground. There. Bootprints. Miles and Niles had emerged from the woods right there. The trail led from the trees, into the meadow, and then stopped. The bootprints vanished. Had they taken off their shoes? They wouldn't have had time. He'd been right on their tails.

Josh shielded his eyes from the sun and scanned the area. A warm breeze ruffled the tops of the grasses. Woodcocks frolicked. A pair of swans paddled placidly in the pond. Chipmunks played chase in the branches of an elm tree. It was disgusting.

Josh walked over to the elm tree and punched it.

A few mikes later, the rest of Papa Company tumbled into the meadow and found their commander standing in the grass, sucking on his knuckles.

"What happened, sir?" asked Mudflap.

Josh took his fingers out of his mouth.

"They disappeared."

Papa Company stood silent in the sunny meadow.

"They just disappeared," said Josh.

The twins had the same question, but neither wanted to ask it.

How the heck can two kids just disappear?

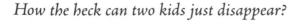

IT'S A PRETTY GOOD QUESTION: How the heck can two kids just disappear?

And the answer is: Sod.

Now: What is sod?

I'm glad you asked!

This is sod:

It's basically a carpet of dirt and grass. Lay it down on the ground and—boom!—now you have a lawn, a football field, or a mini-golf course. There are rolls and rolls of sod for sale at hardware stores, gardening shops, and sod emporiums. Yawnee Valley Feed Supply in downtown Yawnee Valley sells five kinds of sod: bluegrass, Bermuda, tall fescue, dwarf fescue, and meadow mix, which retails at fifty cents a square foot. The day before they disappeared, Niles Sparks, four feet nine inches tall, and Miles Murphy, five foot one, bought ten square feet of sod for five bucks and carried it out to the woods.

HOW TO JUST DISAPPEAR IN 4 EASY STEPS, USING SOD

Step 1: Miles and Niles dug one hole each, as long as they were tall, as wide as they were wide, as deep as they were deep.

"It's like we're digging our own tombs!" said Niles.

"Yikes," said Miles.

Step 2: They covered their holes with sod.

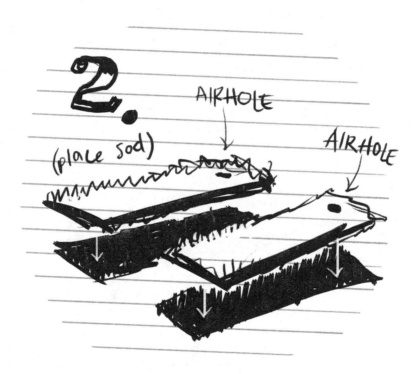

"Make sure you leave a little air tunnel," said Niles. "Otherwise you'll end up buried alive."

"Come on, man!"

Step 3: They each propped up one end of their sod with a big stick, like so:

"Well?" Miles leaned on his shovel. "Anything morbid to say?"

Niles smiled sweetly and ran his fingers across the turf. "Walt Whitman calls grass the uncut hair of graves."

"I don't know who that is, and I don't want to know who that is," said Miles.

Step 4: Twenty-four hours later, with Josh Barkin in hot pursuit, Miles and Niles exploded into the meadow. Niles could feel his lungs beating against his rib cage. He breathed in great gulps but still couldn't get enough air. He hated running.

"Come on!" Miles said.

He'd paused again to let Niles catch up.

Josh was crashing around in the woods behind them.

Miles held out his hand for Niles to slap as he ran by. Together they dashed across the meadow, over to the elm. They threw themselves into their holes and knocked away the sticks. The sod covered their bodies. By the time Josh got to the meadow, Miles and Niles were invisible, lying beneath blankets woven of hopeful green stuff. Sod!

UNDER HIS SOD, surrounded on all sides by damp, rich dirt, Niles could hear Papa Company talking up above:

"Maybe they doubled back into the woods, sir."

"Don't be a nimbus. I would have seen them."

"Maybe they spontaneously combusted, sir."

"I wish."

"Maybe they're up in that elm tree, sir."

"Maybe they doubled back into the woods and you *didn't* see them, sir."

"Maybe they're in the pond, sir."

". . ."

"And they're breathing through snorkels. Or straws. Sir."

"Yeah! Or they're wearing scuba gear, sir!"

"Sir, they could have gotten into a bathysphere that they had parked by the pond, just waiting."

"What's a bathysphere?"

"It's like a submarine."

"Well, why didn't you just say submarine, Mudflap? Bathy-sphere!"

"Ooh! Sir! Maybe they turned into swans!"

"What?"

"Swans. Those swans, sir!"

"There are two of them, sir!"

"They're not wizards, you nimbuses. They're pranksters. They go to my school. A couple nimbuses who call themselves the Terrible Twos."

Underground, Niles rolled his eyes and corrected Josh: "The Terrible *Two*." He said it so softly that only an earthworm, who was crawling near his face, could have heard him, if earthworms had ears, which they don't. They don't have eyes either. Niles wondered whether earthworms had mouths, and especially whether they had teeth, and he hoped they didn't, because now the earthworm was crawling *on* his face. This kind of stuff happens when you're hiding out below the earth.

Anyway, back to Josh:

"They got away from us. But we'll find them. They've been hanging out in the woods all summer. We'll track them down.

We will retake our flag. And we will have our revenge. We will prank them like you wouldn't believe. We will throw sticks at their heads. We will poke them with the sharp parts of these medals. We will fill a sock with oranges and thwomp them. We will prank those pranksters so hard they will never want to prank again."

OBVIOUSLY Josh doesn't really understand what a prank is.)

(But that doesn't make him any less scary.)

(Actually, it probably makes him more scary.)

WHEN THEY WERE SURE the cadets had left the meadow, Miles and Niles rose up out of the ground, gasping fresh air. They had dirt in their hair. They had dirt in their clothes. They had dirt in their mouths.

It was worth it.

They sat in their trenches and laughed. They rested their elbows on the grass and laughed. They laughed so hard they had to lie back down in their holes.

Niles stared up at a cloudless sky. He was completely content, so happy to be relaxing post-prank in the cool earth that he almost forgot to check his watch.

"Ninety-six minutes." He removed a notebook from his pocket and noted the time. It was a record: the longest time spent continuously pranking. Niles recorded stuff like this for a book he was planning, a tome, really: *The History of the*

Terrible Two, which would be for sale in the gift shop of their museum, as well as fine bookstores everywhere.

"You want to get out of these holes? There's a bunch of bugs and worms down here."

"That's redundant," said Niles. "Worms *are* bugs."

"No, bugs are like beetles and flies and stuff. Insects."

Niles thought it over. "Would you say a spider is a bug?" he asked.

"Of course! Classic bug."

"Well, a spider's not an insect. It's an arachnid."

"I know that. Everybody knows that. Don't spoil the occasion."

"What occasion?" Niles asked.

"Our longest consecutive prank."

"You knew!"

Niles smiled.

So did Miles.

They stood up, walked across the meadow, and disappeared into the forest.

LIKE ANY self-respecting outlaws, Miles and Niles had a lair: a cave deep in the woods that only they knew about. To get there, you had to cross a log that a storm had blown over a creek. (The creek wasn't deep—it went up to their calves—but the log was more fun, and who likes wet socks?) A blackberry tangle seemed to block off the way, but a secret path took you safely through brambles, into a ravine that wound down through tall rocks and spilled out into a little green glade with a brook and a cave. The mouth of the cave was in the side of a hill, surrounded by rocks that were covered in moss. The cave wasn't big, but it was their home in the woods: the prank lab west, summer HQ of the Terrible Two.

They spent many days in their cave. Sometimes they slept over out there. Miles's mom didn't really like Niles's parents. She found them "aloof." (She wasn't wrong.) Because Ms. Murphy almost never talked to Mr. and Mrs. Sparks, emancipation was easy. Miles would say he was sleeping at Niles's, and Niles would say he was sleeping at Miles's, and the boys would sneak off, bound for wild blooms, birdsong, and liberty in Yawnee Valley Regional Park and Outdoor Recreational Area.

Their lair was kitted out comfortably: sleeping bags on pads of soft forest grass, flashlights, snacks, books in tall stacks, a rock Miles thought was a fossil but wasn't, a doorknob, feathers from twelve kinds of birds, a ladder, string, a big piece of fool's gold, some animal's leg bones that still bent at the knee (Miles said a coyote, Niles said fox), two duck calls (one each), two chairs, tools, paper and pens, everything you need for croquet, six different board games, a hand-carved chess set, a cigar box containing good skipping stones, blankets, warm hats, and portable speakers so Niles could still play all his tunes.

And now they had a flag.

"It doesn't exactly go with the place, does it?" said Niles.

"No. It freaks me out."

"Yeah."

They stared at the flag for a while.

A *long* while.

Even longer.

"You know, maybe we should turn it around," Miles said.

Miles took the flag from the wall and held it in front of his body.

"It looks like the snake swallowed your body up to the neck, and he's going for your head!" said Niles.

Miles looked down and frowned.

"No. It looks like my skeleton is made of snake bones!"

"How is that any better?"

Miles shrugged. "I don't know. Seems better than being eaten."

"OK."

Miles hung the flag back up backward. Now it was a blank black field on their wall.

"Much better," said Miles.

Niles agreed. "Let's go outside."

An oak tree grew beside the creek. It had spiky leaves, silver bark, and two ropes tied around its trunk. One rope was red, one rope was blue, and both ran from the tree into the stream. Niles tugged on the blue rope, which was tied to a bottle of lemonade submerged in the cool water. Then he pulled the red rope and fished out a bottle of iced tea. The creek kept the drinks cold. Niles poured two Arnold Palmers.

Miles made a toast.

"In victory!"

They clinked their mugs.

The drinks were delicious.

"Oh!" said Niles. "And we have fruit cocktail!"

They spent the afternoon lying in the grass outside their cave, listening to music on their tiny speakers. Niles was playing only songs that had whistling.

"Who's this?" Miles asked.

"Otis Redding," said Niles.

"He's a good whistler," said Miles.

"Yeah," said Niles.

Miles watched his friend listen to the whistling. Niles's eyes were unfocused. He was chewing his lip. Niles was there in the glade, but he was also somewhere else. Miles knew what was going on: He was replaying their prank in his head. He was dissecting it. He was reliving it. He was experiencing their prank as it happened, and versions of their prank that never happened, versions where things went even better, versions where things went horribly awry. After a good prank, Miles felt relaxed. But Niles? Niles stayed keyed up for hours.

"Who's this?" Miles asked.

Niles's eyes refocused.

"Ennio Morricone."

"That's who's whistling?"

"No. That's the composer. Alessandro Alessandroni is who's whistling."

"He's a good whistler," said Miles. "And he's got a good name."

"One of the best whistlers," said Niles. "And one of the best names."

How did Niles know all this stuff? The names of Italian whistlers. What leeks looked like. Walt Whitman. Miles wondered whether he should know all this stuff too. More than that, Miles wondered whether *Niles* thought he should know all this stuff. Was Niles ever disappointed with him? Miles had known Niles for twenty-three months. They'd been best friends for more than half that time. But sometimes he still worried: Why me? Why did Niles choose me to be his best friend?

Niles was moving his mouth now, but no words came out. His face was animated. He was having a conversation with someone who wasn't there, and it looked like an intense one.

Niles sat up and made an announcement.

"He really steams me."

Miles took a guess. "Josh?"

"Yeah! I mean, anybody can call themselves a prankster. But actually pulling a prank? A *real* prank? That's a lot harder. That takes wit. That takes finesse. That takes imagination."

Miles nodded. When Niles got worked up like this, it was best to just let him go.

"So you tell someone to walk up close to you, just so you can throw a stick at his head? Ha ha." (Niles actually said "Ha ha.") "Well. So what? What does that prove? That you can boss people around? Well! Pranks do not belong to the powerful! The prank is too fine an instrument for a brute's clumsy fingers!"

Niles was standing now.

"The prank belongs to the powerless! It is the mustache across the dictator's portrait, the tweak of the tyrant's nose.

Josh Barkin, there's a guy who needs his nose tweaked. He gives pranksters a bad name. He gives Barkins a bad name."

Now that was saying something.

Niles walked over to the creek and stared at the water for a while.

Then he walked back to the grass.

"Also, you can't prank a squirrel. That's not even possible."

Miles nodded.

"OK," said Niles. "I'm done. Thanks for listening."

He sat down and picked up a book he was halfway through. But Niles read only a few sentences before he checked the time and snapped the book shut.

"Gotta go," he said. "I'll be back."

Some days, when they were in the forest, Niles would disappear for an hour or two in the late afternoon. He never said where he went, and Miles never asked. Miles knew that if he did ask, Niles would tell him. But he also figured if Niles wanted to tell him, he would. Niles liked to keep secrets, even from his best friend. And although Miles was curious, he'd also learned to give Niles the privacy he needed, even if he didn't really understand why. Anyway, during that summer they saw each other almost every day, all day. If Miles was being honest, it was nice to get a break. Niles could be intense.

He listened to the song, to the birds, and to the splashing of the brook. Soon he fell asleep.

When Niles returned two hours later, he entered the glade talking. It was like he'd never left.

Miles opened his eyes.

"You know," Niles said, "Josh is going to come for that flag."

"OR WE COULD JUST make a new flag!" said Mudflap.

Papa Company was back in their barracks, having a Squadron Meeting, or SQUADMEET. The way Mudflap saw things, making a new flag had two advantages over recovering their old one: They wouldn't have to spend time out in the wilderness, where there were snakes, and they could put a different animal on the flag, instead of a snake.

"We could grab some art supplies and do it right here, from the comfort of our cabin!"

"*Barracks*," said Splinters.

"Right. Barracks. From the comfort of our barracks!"

Their barracks was a cabin, furnished with a row of uncomfortable beds.

Josh couldn't believe what he was hearing.

"TWENTY PUSH-UPS!" he PLOPped. "That's an order."

"Both of us, sir, or just Mudflap?" asked Splinters.

"Just Mudflap, and now you for asking," said Josh.

Splinters and Mudflap got on the floor and began huffing away at their push-ups.

"There are no *art supplies* here, Mudflap," said Josh. "Look at that activity board. Do you see 'Crafts Time' up there?"

Mudflap lifted his head to look at the schedule on the wall.

"That's not proper push-up form!" Josh yelled. "SNAUSAGES! SNAUSAGES!"

SNAUSAGES was another military acronym Josh had made up, which in Papa Company meant "Straight Neck, Arms Under Shoulders, Angle and Get Elbows Straight," and more generally refers to a popular brand of sausage treats for dogs.

Mudflap laughed and collapsed on the floor.

Josh glared.

The room was utterly silent, except for Mudflap's loud giggling.

"Something funny?" Josh asked.

"Um, yes, sir," said Mudflap. "Snausages."

"Another acronym," said Splinters, mid-push-up.

"Oh. I was thinking of the sausage treats," said Mudflap, and he started giggling again.

"Thirty more push-ups. That's an order. When you're done, *then* you can look up at the activity board and see if it says 'Crafts Time.'"

Mudflap started over at one.

Josh waited for him to do thirty push-ups.

Thirty push-ups is a lot.

Especially when people are staring at you.

So it took a long time.

Josh began to regret assigning the extra push-ups.

"Thirty!" said Mudflap.

"That was only twenty-nine," said Splinters.

Josh punched his bed.

Finally, Mudflap finished, looked at the activity board, and confirmed what you've probably guessed: It included "Running Through a Bunch of Tires," "Extreme Marching," and "Holding Stuff Above Your Head for a While," but not "Crafts Time."

All those push-ups had disrupted the violent momentum Josh had been hoping to generate in this SQUADMEET, so he decided to whip up his troops with a speech. He strode back and forth in the barracks.

"You're darn right it doesn't say 'Crafts Time.' This is not an art camp. There are no art supplies. This is not a drama camp. There is no drama, except for the drama we are currently involved in, the dramatic war we are waging on a couple of dumb nimbuses in the forest. This is not a canoe-around-a-lake camp. Sure, there is a lake right over there, but there are no canoes! This is a boot camp. We have . . . boots! And we are going to use our boots to kick those nimbuses in their heads!"

Mudflap and Splinters whooped enthusiastically. It was a rousing speech, the kind delivered by important generals standing in front of giant flags. (Unfortunately, their flag had been stolen.)

"Those nimbuses took our flag. And when somebody takes something from you, what do you do? Do you go to an art closet and do an art project? No. Like I already mentioned, we don't have an art closet. But more importantly, art is for nim-buses! Except for martial arts, which are awesome. Hi-yah!" Josh kicked the wall of the cabin. "When somebody takes something from you, here is what you do: You go and take that something back! And that is what we will do. Every morning before breakfast, every snack time, every activity period, Papa Company will scour the forest for those two thieves. Boys, this is a RECON mission!"

"Is RECON another acronym?" asked Mudflap.

(RECON is not an acronym. It's short for reconnaissance, because reconnaissance is a tough word to spell correctly.)

"Um," said Josh. "Yes. Yes, RECON is an acronym. Now—"

"What does it stand for?" asked Splinters.

Josh sighed.

"Well . . . it . . . stands for . . ."

Josh stared at the ceiling of his barracks. He felt instinctively that this was an important test of his leadership. Josh firmly believed that good leaders never admit when they don't know something. And the fact was, Josh didn't know what this acronym stood for. (Again, it wasn't an acronym.) He began to blush a pale plum color. This was a tough spot. What could he do?

"RECON stands for . . . Really . . ."

He was off to a good start!

"Enormous . . . Counterstrike . . ."

O. O. O.

"On . . ."

Aha! Josh was almost there. He screwed up his eyes and willed all his blood to his brain. Josh's face darkened and became the shade of a turnip. Just one letter left!

His eyes lit up.

The word came to him like a gift from his ancestors, inscribed in his mind with the ballpoint pen of principals past.

"NIMBUSES!"

His cadets nodded.

Brilliant! That was brilliant. Really Enormous Counterstrike On Nimbuses. It was like poetry. Heck, it wasn't *like* poetry. It *was* poetry. Really Enormous Counterstrike On Nimbuses! That was a work of art! And not dumb art, like whatever flag Mudflap wanted to make, but cool art, like karate. The art of leadership. The art of power. The art of war. Josh had to admit, he had a real knack for acronyms. In fact, at that moment, to commemorate his great accomplishment, Josh invented yet another acronym! It was an acronym to help him remember what to do when he didn't know what an acronym stood for: Deny Ignorance, Make Something Up, Mister, or DIMSUM, which more generally refers to a very tasty cuisine featuring dumplings and steamed buns.

Seeing the unquestioning admiration in his cadets' eyes, it occurred to Josh that he was a genius. And like many people who think they are geniuses, Josh figured he should probably write a book. It would be a book containing all the military acronyms he had made up. And he would call it *The Art of War*, by Josh Barkin. But right now a bugle blew outside the barracks, which meant he had to get changed for swimming.

THE ART OF WAR is already a book and has been for about 2,500 years. It was written by a genius named Sun Tzu, and Niles Sparks had read it. In fact, *The Art of War* was one of the books he'd brought to the prank lab west, and he was scouring the spines stacked up along the walls of the cave, trying to find it.

"Here it is!"

Of course, it was at the bottom of a column that was almost as tall as Niles, beneath books by Dumas and Pyle and Raskin and Dahl and Babbitt and Gannett and Konigsburg and Adams and Borges and Twain and Shakespeare and Scieszka and Stevenson and Shakespeare and Tolkien and Lewis and Fitzhugh and Malory and Cleary.

"Just my luck," said Niles.

"It wouldn't have been a problem if we hadn't brought out so many books." Miles was deep into a project, painting a rock white so it looked like a tooth.

"If we hadn't brought out so many books, we might not have had the *right* book. This book!"

"Uh-huh," said Miles.

"So," said Niles, "will you lift up the rest of these books so I can grab it?"

"Ughhhhhhhhhhhhhhhhhhhhhhhhhh," said Miles, and put down his paintbrush.

"Ughhhhhhhhhhhhhhhhhhhhhhhhhh," Miles continued, walking over to the stack.

"Ugggggggggggggggggggggggggggg," Miles groaned, lifting up thirty-two books. It was a slightly different noise because the books were so heavy.

"Besides," said Niles, "I don't really feel comfortable unless I'm surrounded by my books. It helps me think. Good books are like good pranks: They challenge the

powerful, they expose the truth, and sometimes they're funny."

"Just grab the book, Niles!"

Niles snapped out of his reverie and snatched up *The Art of War*.

A lot of Sun Tzu's advice is specifically for ancient Chinese generals—there's a lot about draft animals and shields—but there's some good stuff for pranksters in there too.

"Listen to this," said Niles. "'Lure with bait; Strike with chaos.'"

"Cool," said Miles.

He went back to work on his fake tooth.

Niles wasn't satisfied with Miles's "cool" but he continued: "Oh, this is so good: 'If I do not wish to engage, I can hold my ground with nothing more than a line drawn around it.'"

Miles looked up. "Niles, what does all this junk mean?"

Niles walked over to a big map of the forest he and Miles had drawn and hung up in their cave.

He took a pencil from behind his ear and drew a circle around their little glade.

"It means," said Niles, "that we've got to build some traps."

Miles stood up and grinned. "Now we're talking!"

It took a flashlit night in their cave to plan the fortifications, and ten days to actually build them.

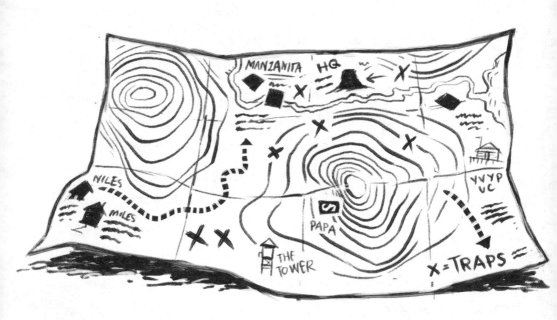

THE WOODS IN SUMMER are full of life. A sharp observer can spot raccoons, opossums, deer, skunks, coyotes, cows (moo), cougars, and, if you're lucky, school principals.

Look, behind the bushes! There's one now:

A wonderful specimen! Brand-new boots. Brand-new socks (bright red—power socks). Brand-new shorts and brand-new backpack. A walking stick that was a very old branch, but as a walking stick was brand-new. A brand-new sunburn (purplish).

This principal's name was Principal Barkin. He was the father of Josh Barkin, and the principal of Yawnee Valley Science and Letters Academy, a school that is not in this book. On this morning, already warm, he leaned on his walking stick and breathed the forest air.

"Ah, wildflowers and cows!" said Principal Barkin to nobody, because he was hiking alone.

He consulted a brand-new compass and a brand-new trail map. He checked the coordinates against a Global Positioning Satellite Hiking Aid, which was very expensive and, yes, brand-new.

"Excellent," he said. "Yes, yes, precisely as I expected."

He surveyed the woods and smiled.

Principal Barkin was lost.

But no matter! A principal is never truly lost. In times of uncertainty, a good leader randomly chooses a direction and pursues it boldly, no matter where it leads. This was a lesson he'd learned from his own father, whom he had complicated feelings about, and a lesson he'd passed on to his son, whom he also had complicated feelings about. But enough feeling! More walking. Principal Barkin spun around and pointed his arm out. West!

He grimaced.

It was a rough path.

But west it would have to be! He pulled up his socks and marched forth, singing a new song he'd made up called "The Ballad of the Wandering Principal":

Fi-diddlee-dee,
No school for me!
It's summer for school principals!
Yes siree, I'm totally free.
A wandering school principal.

Summertime is here again.
School principals are free.
The birds are singing in the trees

And so are the school principals.
Not in the trees, but on the ground.
School principals cannot fly.

But what if they could? That would be neat!
A high-flying school principal!
Climbing high like state test scores
At a school with a good principal.

I'd flap my arms and fly above
The classrooms and gymnasium.
Students would look up at me
And say, "That man's my principal."

And don't forget the faculty!
And staff! And PTA!
I'd be the pride of the whole school!
School, school, school,
School, school, school—
Good gracious, I miss school.

Principal Barkin was lost in more ways than one.

Over hills and through what he assumed were dales, Principal Barkin wandered through the greenwood till he reached a little stream. With his walking stick, he plumbed its depths.

He murmured disapprovingly.

"Not too deep," he said. "But these are brand-new socks."

He scanned up and down the bank, searching for some alternative passage.

"A log!" he exclaimed, startling a family of rabbits. "Thank you, Mother Nature!"

He wobbled as he crossed the log and had to steady himself with his stick. "Look at me!" he cried, once again startling the rabbits, who had just settled back in their burrow. "Crossing a log bridge with a great stick!" For a moment, he felt like a boy again. Not because he'd crossed a lot of log bridges,

or held a lot of sticks, as a kid. No, no, nothing of the kind. In fact, Principal Barkin, then known as Little Barry Barkin, had been forbidden from the forest. His father, then known as Principal Barkin, had a saying: "Nature puts humans in contact with the limits of our power, and should therefore be avoided." But the scene—the stick, the log, the creek— reminded Principal Barkin of the adventure novels he used to read as a boy, late at night, up in his room, books that brought him endless joy—until his father found out and ended the joy, with another saying: "Adventure stories remind us of the hurly-burly that lies beneath the order of everyday life, and are thus unsuitable for children and adults." His father had donated the books to the library of a rival school.

"I wonder," Principal Barkin wondered, "if some jolly fellow will emerge from these woods and try to cross this log in the opposite direction. I would knock him on the crown with my walking stick! And then he'd invite me to join his merry band!"

Of course, he wasn't really expecting a jolly fellow to emerge from the woods, which was good, because one didn't. The rabbits were the only living creatures within earshot, and they were digging deep into the earth, trying to get as far away from this loud man as possible.

Principal Barkin sighed wistfully and continued on his journey.

Soon enough, he reached a bramble patch.

"Blackberries!" said Principal Barkin. He checked his compass. Just as he feared: His path west led right through the thorny bushes. "It's too bad there's not some sort of secret path to get me safely through these brambles." (There was one: As you've probably guessed, this is the blackberry patch described on page 68. Principal Barkin didn't know about the secret path, though, because it was secret.)

"Ah well!" said Principal Barkin. "I will traverse this briar patch like a fox!" And this he did, suffering many painful nicks and cuts.

"Ouch!" said Principal Barkin. "I'll just—aw yeep! OK, maybe if I turn back and oh ooh no goodness!"

He was glad to make it to the other side of the brambles, and even gladder when his path westward led him through a ravine and into a little green glade.

"Look at that brook! Look at that cave! I mean, is this Yawnee Valley Regional Park and Outdoor Recreational Area or a fairy bower?" It was a rhetorical question, which was good, because nobody was around to answer it. Still, even though he knew he was in Yawnee Valley Regional Park and Outdoor

Recreational Area, Principal Barkin couldn't help imagining a fairy queen awakening to the sound of his voice, and falling madly in love with him, and assigning several fairy children to dote on him. "Fetch me some honey," he'd say to the fairy children, and also, "Why aren't you in school?" And they would tell him that there wasn't any such thing as a school for fairies. And he would say, "Outrageous!" And he would build them a school, out of sticks and acorns and things, a place where the fairies would learn, and he would be their school principal. And the fairy queen would ask him to be her king, and he would say, "No, no, my lady. A principal is all I am, and all I ever wanted to be." But she'd make him king anyway.

"Well," said Principal Barkin. He suddenly remembered that he should call his wife, Mrs. Barkin, if he ever found some cell service in this forest.

Principal Barkin decided that the glade would be an enchanting spot to rest awhile, so he strolled across the grass and promptly fell into a large hole.

ON THE SAME DAY, at almost the same time, in a different part of the woods, another Barkin, Josh Barkin, was gloating. He was gloating quietly. This was difficult for him, because he was by nature a loud gloater. But his current situation demanded stealth. The situation was this: crouching behind a shrub, spying on Miles Murphy and Niles Sparks.

He'd found them! After two weeks of patrols in the forest, klick after klick of tromping through plants, slapping mosquitoes, drinking water that had been warmed up in his canteen and so felt really gross in his mouth, Josh Barkin had

practically stumbled right over those two nimbuses. No. Not stumbled. Josh Barkin had *precisely targeted* those two nimbuses. He considered signaling Splinters and Mudflap, who were scouting elsewhere, but he didn't want to risk attracting attention, plus he'd assigned the cadets parts of the forest that were far away and pretty hard to get to.

The whistling had given Miles and Niles away. Josh had heard whistling near a shady spot under the tree he'd been patrolling, and he went to investigate. Josh had found Miles and Niles merrily hiking a path that ran near Yawnee Valley Yelling and Push-Ups Camp. (The area right by camp was Josh's territory to patrol.) They were carrying a ladder, like a couple of dorks. The ladder clanged. The boys whistled. These nimbuses were not stealthy at all. And now they would lead him right back to their headquarters. Pshh. The Terrible Two. More like . . . the Terrible at Hiding Two. Josh chuckled at his own joke, then angrily shushed himself. Miles and Niles were getting ahead of him, so he left his cover and crept after them.

Miles whistled.

"Oooh, that was a good one!" said Niles.

Niles whistled back, and the boys both started laughing.

"I can't get the notes right," Niles said.

"That's true," said Miles, "you can't."

Niles carried the front of the ladder, while Miles carried the back.

"How do you do it?" Niles asked. "How do you control the notes?"

Miles shrugged. "I just do it. With my mouth muscles."

"Yeah, but *how*? Describe *how*."

"I can't describe it. I just do it. I guess I'm a prodigy."

"Hmmm," said Niles. He tried whistling again, and then they both started laughing.

"What the heck kind of secret army signal is this?" Josh thought from behind a new shrub. "They don't sound like turkey vultures, or any other kind of bird."

(Miles and Niles weren't practicing secret army signals. They were trying to whistle like Alessandro Alessandroni.)

Niles dropped his end of the ladder and pointed at a tall tree just off the path.

"Look! That's one!"

Miles dropped his end of the ladder. They both ran over to the tree and peered up into its branches.

"This is a jack pine?" Miles asked.

"Yeah!" said Niles.

"It looks just like a normal tree."

"Yeah, it *looks* like it. On the *surface*."

Miles rolled his eyes. "Oh boy."

"Do you have that pocketknife?" Niles asked.

Miles reached into his pocket and got his knife. Niles used it to pry off some bark from the trunk of the tree.

"I don't know, man," Miles said.

"No, it's true. It has something to do with the minerals in the ground that make them grow."

"OK," said Miles.

"You'll see," said Niles.

Niles kept stripping bark from the tree. Josh had no idea what the little nimbus was up to, but whatever it was, it was not going well. As Niles grew more and more frustrated, he pulled off the pieces at a furious pace. Miles began whistling again. Niles glared at him.

"Sorry," said Miles.

Josh wished Miles and Niles would just give up and head back to their secret headquarters, so he could beat them up and steal his flag back.

"Boomtown!" said Niles.

The little blond nimbus had pried off a piece of bark and pulled a fat gold nugget right out of the tree.

Miles's eyes got wide.

Josh's eyes got wider.

"Wow," said Miles.

Niles held the nugget between his thumb and forefinger. "Told you. These trees only grow where there's gold in the ground. It gets stuck in their bark when they're shooting up through the dirt. There should be even more nuggets up higher."

"Let me see that," said Miles. He took his knife back. The boys set their ladder against the pine. Miles climbed up until he reached its lowest branches, which stuck straight out from the trunk a good twelve feet above the ground. Miles hopped from limb to limb until he reached a sturdy bough. He shimmied to the spot where branch met trunk and, his legs wrapped tightly around the bough, began to work at the bark with his knife.

It wasn't long before Miles cackled gleefully.

"Look at this!"

Miles tossed a nugget down to Niles.

It was even bigger than the first one.

"How much do you think that's worth?" Miles asked.

Josh was wondering the exact same thing.

"I don't know," Niles said. "A lot."

"Well, there's more up here. A lot more. We should have brought a backpack."

"We could go back to HQ and get mine," Niles said.

Miles sat high in the tree and thought about it.

"All right," he said. "But let's hurry."

Josh Barkin's mouth was open wide. His heart was beating fast. His face was purpling splotchily. He watched Miles Murphy shimmy down the tree and slide down the ladder, which his little friend held steady with two hands. The boys hurried off away from the trail, into the woods.

They'd left their ladder leaning against the tree.

This was a dilemma.

"Think!" Josh thought. He had two options.

PLAN 1.

(FOLLOW NIMBUSES TO THEIR HEADQUARTERS.)

(TAKE FLAG BACK.)

(BEAT THEM UP.)

(COME BACK TO TREE AND STEAL THEIR GOLD.)

That was a pretty great plan.

But! There was also Plan Two!

PLAN 2.

(TAKE GOLD NOW.)

(HIDE AND WATCH THEM DISCOVER GOLD IS GONE!)

(FOLLOW THEM BACK TO THEIR HEADQUARTERS AND TAKE BACK FLAG.)

(BEAT THEM UP.)

That was also a great plan! How could he decide?

Josh's mom always said Josh was the kind of kid who "would rather eat his dessert first." But what was the dessert here? Stealing a bunch of gold, or beating up a couple of nimbuses? They were both dessert! And you know what, Josh's mom was wrong. He wouldn't rather eat his dessert first. He'd rather eat his dessert first *and* last. Otherwise you're just eating something gross like carrots at the end of the night, when you should be eating dessert. In fact, why eat carrots at all? Why not just eat *all* dessert? And that was the great thing about the options that lay before him: They were all dessert!

"Stop thinking!" Josh thought. At Yawnee Valley Yelling and Push-Ups Camp, campers were expected to be A-OK— Action-Oriented Kids. Hiding behind a shrub, cooking up food metaphors, was *not* Action-Oriented. It felt like something his father would do. (Josh was probably right about that.) And Josh did not want to be like his father! It was time to stop thinking about dessert and time to start eating dessert! And Plan Two had an extra step, which was like more dessert, so he would eat that plan!

He stood up.

He was a little hungry.

But he had firmly decided on Plan Two.

(Good thing: Miles and Niles had left so long ago it'd be hard to follow them at this point.)

Josh clambered up the ladder and lifted himself into the tree. Now. Where had that nimbus been digging around with his knife? Josh spied a spot where the trunk was scratched and stripped. It was five feet above his head. That nimbus could climb, Josh would give him that. But so could Josh. Yawnee Valley Yelling and Push-Ups Camp wasn't just about push-ups. There were also a lot of pull-ups, and so Josh had no trouble pulling himself up the pine branches.

Wow. He was up pretty high. Hugging a branch high above the ground sure didn't feel like dessert. But he hadn't gotten to the gold yet. Josh grinned and shimmied along the bough. He kept his pocketknife sheathed in his boot, under his sock, because it looked cooler when he took it out. At least it looked cool when he was on the ground. Getting his foot up to his hand without falling out of the tree took some awkward twisting. But so what? Nobody was watching him. If a kid almost falls out of a tree in the forest, and nobody is there to see him, is it embarrassing? Well, what do you think?

Anyway, Josh managed to grab the knife.

"Aw yeah," said Josh. He stabbed the tree.

He jimmied the handle and got some bark off. No gold. He stabbed it again and pried off a pretty big piece. There was no gold underneath, just more bark. Obviously, this work required patience.

Ten mikes later, he still hadn't found any gold and was just stabbing the tree out of anger. Miles had said there was a bunch of gold up here. "Do those nimbuses know some trick I don't?" He stared at his knife, wiped the blade on his shorts to get the sap off, then stabbed the tree again.

"Hullo, Josh!" said Niles, down on the ground.

"Hello, Josh!" said Miles, who was also on the ground, and who thought it was funny how Niles had said "hullo" but wasn't sure that he'd be able to pull it off. "You look like a plum up there!"

Josh squeezed his thighs tight against the branch but otherwise managed to play it cool. "What do you nimbuses want?"

"Good-bye, Josh!" said Niles.

"Yeah, bye, Josh!" said Miles.

They took the ladder from the tree and began to walk away with it.

This is bad, thought Josh.

This is really bad, he thought.

This is really really bad.

(It's not easy to think at the same time you're realizing you're stuck high in a jack pine.)

"You nimbuses may have the ladder," Josh shouted, "but I'm up here with all your gold!"

The boys stopped. Niles turned toward Josh and gave him a disappointed look.

"Josh."

"Oh," said Josh. "Right."

(It was just dawning on Josh that the entire thing had been a prank, but seriously: It's hard to think when you're up a tree, especially when a light breeze has picked up, and the bough you're on trembles.)

Miles and Niles turned to leave once again.

"But how do you get gold in a tree?" Josh shouted after them.

"We stuck a nugget in there yesterday!" said Niles.

"Oh," said Josh. "I know!"

Josh felt the need to establish his dominance in these woods, which had perhaps been diminished by his current predicament. "Whatever!" he said. "Now when I find you, I'll

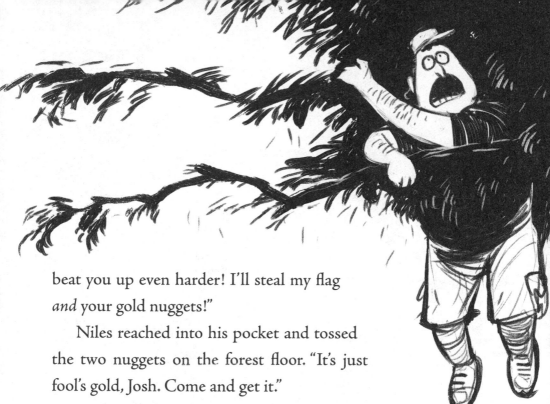

beat you up even harder! I'll steal my flag
and your gold nuggets!"

Niles reached into his pocket and tossed
the two nuggets on the forest floor. "It's just
fool's gold, Josh. Come and get it."

And with that, the Terrible Two marched off,
Miles whistling a carefree tune.

Josh looked down.

There were no branches lower than twelve feet off
the ground.

That was too far to fall.

Josh screeched like an angry turkey vulture, which was
Papa Company's secret distress signal. But soon he decided
there was no need to be discreet. "Help!" he cried. "Help!"

MILES AND NILES had planned on a leisurely stroll back to their hideout. They wanted to revisit all the best moments from their recent successful caper, then spend some time on one of their summer projects: learning to identify every tree in the forest. Yawnee Valley Regional Park and Outdoor Recreational Area was home to more than two hundred different kinds of hardwood trees, each one beautiful in its own distinct way. It would take many pages of this book to catalog the trees the boys passed—even longer with adjectives. Unfortunately, there's no time for our sylvan interlude. The Terrible Two had only just started reviewing their prank—Niles was doing a devastatingly accurate impression of Josh Barkin— when the sound of a bell rang through the trees, which included cottonwood, box elder, and quaking aspen.

Miles and Niles dropped their ladder and ran toward the bell.

PRINCIPAL BARKIN found himself at the bottom of a hole. By some stroke of luck, his fall had been broken by a thick cushion of hay. He buried his nose in the straw, inhaled its grassy smell, and sighed. It reminded him of his brother's dairy farm. His brother was named Bob, and he was a smug, unscrupulous man, but his farm smelled nice. Principal Barkin especially enjoyed visiting the dairy farm during haymaking season, when fragrant alfalfa lay drying in great piles beside Bob's barn.

It then occurred to Principal Barkin that hay was not a natural thing to find in forests. Moreover, holes were not a natural thing to find in forests! A hole full of hay, well, that was exceedingly uncommon. It was *unnatural.*

And why hadn't he noticed the hole? He'd simply been walking across a patch of grass when the ground had just given way. That was certainly unnatural as well! Unnatural and irregular! He got on his hands and knees and felt around on the ground.

"What the sod?" he said, staring at a handful of sod. The hole had been camouflaged. Barkin realized that he was in a trap.

"A bear trap!" said Principal Barkin. He chuckled. It was fitting. On staff training days, he loved making teachers introduce themselves and then say an animal that began with the same letter as their last name. It was a great icebreaker! Principal Barkin always led by example: "Principal Barkin Bear." And then Ms. Shandy Stingray, Coach O. Ocelot, etc., etc., and so on, and so on. A smile flickered across Principal Barkin's face. Down in his hole, he wondered what the rest of his faculty was up to this summer, and if any of them were having great adventures, like getting stuck in a bear trap.

Anyway! There were plenty of other animals that started with the letter *B*. Buffalo, for one. Bunny, for two. Burro, which was Spanish! But in the icebreaker, Principal Barkin always chose Bear because he felt he was very much like a bear, specifically a Kodiak bear, which was the best bear, and the most powerful.

Well, now he just had to wait until the hunter who set this trap returned and found Barry Barkin down here instead of a bear. A principal in a pit! Wouldn't that be a surprise! Not knowing how long he'd be there, Principal Barkin pulled a bag

of trail mix from his pack. He'd prepared it using a family recipe: all nuts, no chocolate. Principal Barkin's grandfather had
invented the snack and named it "Barkin Gorp." His father,
mistakenly believing that "gorp" was an acronym for "Good
Old Raisins and Peanuts," had renamed it "Barkin Scroggin,"
since it didn't have raisins either. (Gorp is actually an old word
that means "eat greedily." That's the kind of surprising fact
you might learn in the middle of a story about adventures in
the woods, but of course Principal Barkin's father didn't read
those.)

Principal Barkin was gorping his scroggin when he noticed
the bell.

There was a bell in the hay, partially obscured by some sod!
That was odd, and this was even odder: The bell had a note
attached.

Since bears cannot read, Barkin immediately revised his

assessment: This was a mantrap! Or perhaps it would be better to say "human trap"! Although in this particular case, he was a man, and "human trap" lacked a certain ring, so, yes, a mantrap! The bell, the note, the hay, the sod, the fact that the top of the hole was just beyond his reach, the reach of a man— it all made sense!

But who would set a mantrap in the woods? A jolly fellow seeking a school principal to round out his merry band? A fairy queen seeking a school principal to round out her woodland court? An insane hermit seeking a school principal to round out a balanced breakfast?

Principal Barkin hoped it wasn't the last one and gave the bell a ring.

MILES AND NILES peered down into one of their traps and were surprised to find their school principal peering back.

"Ah." Principal Barkin was chagrined. "I should have known. The Terrible Twos."

"The Terrible Two," said Miles.

"The Terrible Two," said Principal Barkin.

Niles was quiet. He was lost in his own mind. At this moment, one Barkin was stuck in a tree while another one was stuck underground, and the symmetry of the situation tickled Niles's brain. For Niles, pranking was an art, and he had an artist's appreciation of a beautiful accident.

"What are you doing down there?" Miles asked.

Back when he had suspected Miles Murphy to be a prankster but believed Niles Sparks to be a model student, Principal Barkin had liked Niles much better than Miles. Now that he knew that Miles and Niles were both pranksters, he still preferred Niles.

"That is a question I should be asking you, Miles Murphy, even though I already know the answer, which is that I am obviously once again the intended victim of one of your ridiculous pranks. I seem to be stuck in a principal trap."

"We're not trying to catch principals," Miles said.

"You're not?" Principal Barkin brightened. "Well, I must say that I am pleased to hear it, since I'd hoped we'd gotten over our unfortunate dynamic after our last adventure," said Principal Barkin, referring to a bunch of stuff from book two, "although I'm realizing now that we never made it clear what our relationship would be going forward, whether we remain antagonists, or whether we had joined together in a new and permanent secret supersociety called the Terrible Threes—"

"Three," said Miles.

"Yes, joined together in a new and permanent secret supersociety, the Terrible Three—"

"We definitely didn't do that," said Miles.

Principal Barkin frowned. "Of course not. Well, I suppose we'll sort all that out once school starts again."

"You mean we're not in trouble, Principal Barkin?" Niles asked.

"No! This is not a principal trap, and, since it is summer, I am technically not even your principal, so you should probably call me Barry."

"But, Barry—" said Miles.

"I invited Niles to call me Barry," said Principal Barkin, "not you, Miles."

"But, Principal Barkin," said Miles, "I thought a principal was a principal always, even on Sundays."

"Who said that?"

"You did."

Principal Barkin nodded. "Sounds like me. Wise words. Very wise words. But, Miles, you need to loosen up! We're not talking about Sundays—we're talking about the *summertime*. I mean, who knows what day of the week it is!"

(It was Sunday.)

"Plus, we are in the woods, boys! There are no rules in the woods, besides whatever rules the Yawnee Valley Park District enforces, hold on, I grabbed a brochure from a little ranger station in the parking lot and put it somewhere in my backpack, ah, here it is, wow, that's a lot of rules. But these are mostly rules about fire safety! I am talking about the rules of society! In the woods, boundaries dissolve. There are no pedestals that elevate principals high above students, which is a principal's rightful place in town. There are no obstacles separating father and son, even if that son is surly and disrespectful, partly because of hormones, probably, although sometimes I worry that there is more going on there, a darkness that I just can't seem to . . ."

Principal Barkin trailed off.

"Are you talking about Josh?" asked Niles.

"Josh Barkin? No! Just a hypothetical father and son. In any case, the woods are a natural place for a couple of rapscallions like yourselves. Out here, everything gets turned on its head! Thus I find myself looking up at you, Miles Murphy, whereas in school I am always looking down at you, both metaphorically, in the sense that I disapprove of your general attitude and manner of dress, especially your T-shirts, and literally, in the sense that I am much taller than you. Out here, I couldn't punish you if I wanted to, which I don't."

Principal Barkin was surprised to hear himself speak this sentence, and even more surprised that it felt true.

"Now," said Principal Barkin, "how do I get out of this hole?"

"We had a ladder," said Niles, "but we left it back in the forest."

"Ah," said Principal Barkin. "I see."

And so Miles and Niles reached down into the hole. Miles grabbed Principal Barkin's right arm with both his hands, and Niles grabbed Principal Barkin's left hand with both his hands, and they pulled. Principal Barkin used his legs to scramble up the side of the pit, and the boys lifted their principal up.

"We did it!" said Principal Barkin.

He looked back down into the hole.

"But may I ask: Why did you set this trap," he asked, "if not to prank me?"

"We don't *just* prank you, Principal Barkin."

"Right," said Principal Barkin. "Of course."

"We dug this hole for defense," said Miles.

"Defense?"

Niles gave Miles a look like, *Should we tell him?*

Miles gave Niles a look like, *Yeah, it's kind of weird that we would tell him, but yeah.*

"It's a fortification. This area is our base."

"Your base!" Principal Barkin was delighted. "But who would attack your base?"

Niles gave Miles a look like, *We probably shouldn't tell him everything, though.*

"Some kids," said Miles. "We took their flag and they're trying to get it back."

"A giant game of capture the flag in the woods! It's a shame you aren't friends with my son, Josh Barkin. This is just the kind of thing he would love. Although knowing Josh, he'd probably take things too far. To be honest, I really don't know what he would love anymore. But! It's the kind of thing I would have loved, when I was a boy, if my father had allowed me into these woods, which he didn't. Your fathers allow you into these woods?"

"Sure," said Niles.

"My mom does," said Miles. "It's just me and her."

"Oh," said Principal Barkin. "Right. Yes. I'm sorry."

Miles shrugged. "It's fine."

"Well, anyway! These fortifications are ingenious."

Niles smiled. "The skillful warrior does not rely on the enemy's not coming, but on preparedness."

"Who said that?" Principal Barkin asked. "Was that me again?"

"Sun Tzu."

"Oh. Well. It's still very wise."

He checked his brand-new hiking pocket watch. "Well, boys, I should probably be heading off."

"Where are you going?" Miles asked.

"West!"

"What's west?"

"Oh," said Principal Barkin. "I don't know."

"Barry," asked Niles, "what are you doing out here?"

"That's a very good question, Niles."

Principal Barkin sat down on a rock.

"Every summer, my son, Josh Barkin, and I spend two weeks out here. It's our annual Father-Son Outdoor Barkin Bonding Experience! This

year, Josh declined. He couldn't make it, because he is at a summer camp, which I believe is actually not too far from here! Anyway, I then invited my wife, Mrs. Barkin, for a first annual Husband-Wife Outdoor Barkin Bonding Experience! She also declined. She doesn't really like the outdoors. But I had already rented the cabin and spent quite a lot of money on some brand-new camping equipment. And so I am on the first day of my first annual Barry-Barry Outdoor Barkin Bonding Experience! I am exploring these woods, and myself, and when you're exploring, whether nature or yourself, you never know what you will stumble upon, your base, for instance, and that hole, although to be completely frank I was hoping to stumble upon my cabin, and eat some lunch."

"Wait, are you staying at the Manzanita Cabin?" Miles asked.

"I am!"

"You're going in the wrong direction. It's that way a couple miles."

"Well, it appears I will miss lunch!" Principal Barkin shook his plastic baggie. "Don't worry about me, boys, I've got some Barkin Scroggin to tide me over on my way."

"Scroggin?" Miles asked.

"It means trail mix! Carefully prepared according to my family recipe: peanuts, almonds, cashews, and pecans!"

"That sounds like what just comes in a can of mixed nuts," said Niles.

"Yes!" Principal Barkin tapped the side of his head. "But not in the *right proportions*."

Miles and Niles didn't even need to give each other a look.

"Principal Barkin," said Miles, "do you want to have lunch with us?"

Principal Barkin had a rule: Never eat lunch in front of students. He firmly believed that letting students see him eat would diminish his authority. He was not one of those faculty members who dined in the cafeteria because they wanted to "relate to students." Nor did he eat in the teachers' lounge, because a principal needed to wield power not just over students, but over staff as well. No. During the school year, Principal Barkin ate in his office, alone: a principal power lunch.

But school was out. And hadn't he just given a remarkably good speech about rules in the forest?

"What are you having?" asked Principal Barkin.

And that's how Miles, Niles, and Principal Barkin came to sit on a blanket in a little green glade, enjoying a lunch of tomato sandwiches and sugar cereals. It was truly the kind of thing that could happen only in the woods.

"These Arnold Palmers are ice cold!" said Principal Barkin. "Delicious!"

AFTER LINGERING FOR A WHILE after lunch,
Barkin took his leave of the boys. And he took his time
taking his leave. "OK, GOOD-BYE, YOU TWO RUF-
FIANS!" he stood up and said. "I SHOULD BE GOING,
UNLESS OF COURSE YOU WANT TO GIVE ME A
TOUR OF YOUR CAVE!" After the tour he bid them fare-
well—"FAREWELL, PRANKSTERS!"—but stayed a little
longer for a post-lunch snack. Finally he left, but not before
standing at the edge of the glade, waving, and saying, "WELL,
BOYS, IF YOU NEED ME, LIKE I SAID EARLIER,
I'LL BE OVER AT THE MANZANITA CABIN, BUT
OOPS, MAYBE I SHOULDN'T HAVE MENTIONED
IT, SINCE YOU'RE LIABLE TO SNEAK OVER AND
PRANK ME!"

"It's almost like he wants to be pranked," Miles said, after
they were sure Principal Barkin was gone.

"I think he does," said Niles.

"Yeah," said Miles. "But why?"

"I think maybe he's lonely," said Niles. "I mean, a prank can be a slap or a high five. When you and I prank each other, it's because we're friends."

"It's about respect," said Miles.

"Yeah," said Niles. "And affection!"

"OK," said Miles, who felt like affection was a weird word to use, but also a good one. "Still, Principal Barkin hates pranks."

"I think he's changing," said Niles.

Miles frowned. "But he's a *grown man*."

They sat and thought about their principal for a while.

Miles was the first to speak up.

"Well, it was nice seeing him. And weird."

Niles nodded. "It's weird to see your principal wearing shorts."

"Yeah," said Miles. "It's weird seeing a teacher outside of school at all. But even weirder in the summer. You know? In the summer it seems like the teachers shouldn't even *exist*. Like the school shouldn't even exist. Me and my mom drove past it last week on the way to the dentist, and I didn't even recognize the building. The yard was empty, and the parking lot was empty, and the gate was all chained up. And even

though you couldn't see through the walls, you could just tell the whole building was empty. It was like a dead body—everything looked the same, but something important was missing."

"Creepy," said Niles.

"It *was* creepy," said Miles. "I mean, think about it—everybody we know from school, they're all having summers too. Like, have you thought about Stuart at all the last couple months?"

"No."

"Me neither! I love that guy! And just now is the first time I've thought about him since school ended. What's Stuart doing this summer?"

"I think he said his family was going to Australia," said Niles.

"That's what I'm talking about!" Miles was getting excited now. "We're here in the forest, and Stuart is in Australia right now, shouting at a kangaroo."

"HEY!" said Niles, doing his best Stuart impersonation. "That KANGAROO has a POUCH!"

Miles laughed.

(It was a pretty good impersonation.)

"HEY," said Miles, "there's a JOEY in THERE!"

Niles laughed.

(It wasn't a great Stuart impression but it was still pretty funny.)

"Yeah!" said Miles. "Like, what is Scotty up to?"

Niles frowned. "I don't really know Scotty that well."

"Me neither," said Miles. "Still, it feels like he's always around when we're at school. And now he's off somewhere . . . just . . . being Scotty. Which is crazy. I mean, it seems like the world doesn't even exist in the summer, especially when we're out here. Like it's just the two of us. And Josh. And now Principal Barkin. But what's Holly up to, you know? Have you thought about Holly since the last day of school?"

Niles smiled. But he didn't answer.

IN FACT, Niles *had* thought of Holly since the last day of school. And he knew exactly what she was up to. Every few days, in the afternoon, Niles had been leaving the little green glade to meet up with Holly at a swimming hole in the woods.

Niles didn't say anything about these meetings when Miles mentioned Holly. It would have gone against the general thrust of the point Miles was trying to make about summer, which Niles thought was a good one. Plus Niles liked having secrets.

He went to visit Holly that very afternoon.

The swimming hole was a deep pool of cool clear water

encircled by big jagged rocks. There was a big gray goose who lived there during the summer. The goose was the reason most people avoided the swimming hole. He honked and charged at most visitors, but he seemed to like Holly.

Holly didn't go to the swimming hole to swim. She liked to take off her shoes and read with her feet in the water. And when Niles visited, he put his feet in the water and read books with her.

When Holly heard Niles, she looked up from her book.

(It was *Frankenstein*, by Mary Shelley.)

When the goose heard Niles, he honked aggressively.

"Oh hush, you," said Holly.

The goose shut his beak but eyed Niles warily.

"Hey, Butch," said Holly. "How's Sundance?"

"What?" said Niles.

"From a movie." Holly sighed.

"Right!" said Niles. "What movie?"

Holly told him the title, and he wrote it down in his pranking notebook. He tried to watch the movies Holly mentioned because (1) they were usually great movies, and (2) nobody ever caught Holly's movie references, and Niles wanted to be an exception.

"Got it," said Niles.

"How's Miles?" Holly asked.

Niles smiled. "He's great!"

Then he took out his book (it was *The Once and Future King*, by T. H. White), and he took off his shoes and his socks. He sat down next to Holly, and they read.

In the chapter Niles was reading, a boy was turned into a falcon and spent the night in a mews among several cruel and warlike birds. It gave Niles a lot to think about, so he stopped reading and starting thinking, while staring at his feet.

Holly wiggled her toes.

"School's starting up pretty soon," she said.

"Yeah," said Niles. It was late afternoon and the sun was still high in a cloudless sky. It was hard to believe that this day would ever end, let alone the summer. Niles didn't want to think about school, not this afternoon. So he tried not to.

Of course, the harder you try not to think about something, the more you tend to think about it. For example: Don't think of a cow. Try very, very hard not to think of a cow. Empty your mind of anything resembling a cow. Just in case you need help knowing what not to think about, here is what a cow looks like:

"COW"
(Bos taurus)

So don't picture one of those.

OK. Now go for it. Don't think of a cow!

What did you think about?

Was it a cow?

If yes, you understand what Niles was going through. If no, please draw a picture of whatever you did think about on a postcard and mail it to HUMAN BRAIN STUDY, c/o AMULET BOOKS. (The address is on the last page.) Your contribution will help our understanding of science!

Anyway, Niles was having so much trouble not thinking about school that he got up and, wearing all his clothes, jumped into the water.

There was a great splash, and when Niles resurfaced, his hair was plastered flat to the top of his head.

The goose honked.

Holly laughed.

"What the heck, Niles?"

"I needed to short-circuit my brain!" Niles said.

"You know," she said, "I used to think you were a real weirdo. And now that I'm getting to know you, I think you're a completely different kind of weirdo."

Niles smiled. He liked that a lot.

Holly set down her book. She dove into the water.

Niles was delighted. "I want to learn how to do that!"

Holly tried to teach Niles to dive, but the lessons didn't

take. (Niles was too protective of his brain to go headfirst.) So they spent an hour just swimming.

Splinters and Mudflap couldn't believe they had to spend sixty mikes watching the target swim with a girl. First of all, it was obvious the target had a crush on her, and who wanted to watch a woodland romance? Second of all, they had to spend the whole time hidden behind a rock, and their muscles were starting to cramp from staying still. Third of all, they were supposed to be back at camp. But they doubted Josh would punish them, not when they came back with news of their successful patrol. No, Josh would probably reward them! Maybe

he'd even give them some medals! Or order Papa Company to give a parade in their honor! A small parade, yes. But a parade nonetheless!

At 1700 hours, the target and the girl got out of the water.

At 1702, the target picked up his book and his backpack and headed toward a trail opposite their rock.

The girl sat down and picked up her book.

The girl was stationed between them and the target.

As was the goose.

There was no way they could follow the target without being seen.

"See you in three days? Same time, same place?" asked the target.

"Make it noon," said the girl.

"Noon it is," said Niles.

Niles started down the path.

Holly opened her book again, but she stared down at the same page for minutes, smiling.

(She wasn't reading. She was thinking. There's not much to smile at in the second half of *Frankenstein*.)

"Great, more romance," Splinters whispered to his brother.

Mudflap made a gagging sign.

Splinters rolled his eyes into his head like he was dead.

Then they checked their watches, which were synchronized, and melted back into the forest.

OH, HOW JOSH PLOPPED that afternoon. He was positively purple and throwing a fit. The sun was low in the sky and a chilly breeze was rising—perfect swimming weather. At Yawnee Valley Yelling and Push-Ups Camp, swimming worked a little differently: Cadets lined up on a dock while counselors strode around, screaming hurtful things at them, then throwing them in the lake. As a junior counselor, Josh got to toss the smallest campers into the water.

"YOU THINK YOU'RE REALLY FUNNY, BUT ALL YOUR JOKES ARE OUT OF A JOKE BOOK, SCOTTY," he yelled, right in one kid's face. The kid, Scotty—who was a different Scotty from the one in the first two Terrible Two books—nodded sadly as he flew into the lake.

"YOU SAY YOU PREFER THE WAY VELCRO SHOES LOOK, BUT I THINK YOU DON'T KNOW HOW TO TIE YOUR SHOES, JACKSON," he yelled at Jackson, who really did just prefer the look of Velcro.

"Sir, I do so know how to tie my—" Jackson said before landing hard in the water.

"YOU LOOK DUMB WHEN YOU RUN, DARIUS," he yelled at Darius.

"I pronate, sir," Darius said. Right before camp, his mom had bought him some orthotics, custom inserts that Darius put in his shoes. The orthotics were supposed to make it so Darius's knees didn't knock together when he ran, but so far they just made his knees hurt.

"Pronate this," said Josh, who didn't know what pronate meant. He lifted Darius above his head and turned around in a circle, which was the signature move of General Anxiety, Josh's favorite professional wrestler.

Darius was also a big General Anxiety fan, so he knew what was coming next: Josh was going to throw him into the lake, face-first.

And that is exactly what Josh did.

Josh brought a special fury to his responsibilities that evening. He was in a foul mood. His yelling was extra insulting, his throwing extra hard. To the cadets bobbing in the water, today's swimming exercises felt *personal*.

They wondered if Josh was angry with them. The truth was, Josh was angry with himself. Miles and Niles had eluded his grasp. Those nimbuses had embarrassed him. He'd failed in front of Mudflap and Splinters. After telling his lackeys he'd avenge the theft of their flag, he'd ended up stuck in a tree. He had waited up there for over an hour that morning, until finally Mudflap and Splinters had found him. Were they amused to find their leader perched on a branch like a turkey—not a turkey vulture, which was a scary bird, but a turkey-turkey, which is a silly bird that sometimes flies into trees and then forgets how to fly down? Yes, they might have been amused. There was definitely a sort of amused gleam in their eyes when Josh ordered them back to camp to get help.

They had returned accompanied by the supreme commander, who brought a ladder with him. (The supreme commander was what everyone called the man who ran Yawnee Valley Yelling and Push-Ups Camp. His real name was Tim.) Had Mudflap and Splinters chortled when Josh climbed down the ladder? It was hard to say. They had been standing behind his back, and Josh was focused on clambering down the rungs with dignity. But he had definitely heard some noises that sounded like chortling. Josh could tell you who had not chortled, though: the supreme commander. The supreme commander had not been in a chortling mood. No, he had been in a yelling mood, and he'd yelled at Josh for more than thirty mikes, right there in front of Mudflap and Splinters. It had been humiliating.

For the last week, Josh had been observing his lackeys closely for signs of mutiny. He looked for gleams. He listened for chortles. Having become accustomed to the adoration of his underlings, Josh could not bear losing their respect. They certainly would have respected Josh if they could see him now, tossing all these kids into the lake. But they couldn't see him, because they hadn't shown up for swimming, possibly because they no longer respected him. A spotty attendance record was a definite sign of mutiny.

Darius pulled himself up onto the dock.

Josh pushed him back in the water.

"Aw man," cried Darius.

Would it have been any comfort to Darius if he'd known the reason Josh insulted them so personally, and tossed them in the water so brutally, had nothing to do with him, and everything to do with Josh: his fear, his embarrassment, his self-doubt?

Not at all. Darius's nose was full of water and his knees hurt.

Josh should have never promised revenge. He should have just let those nimbuses take his dumb flag. Mudflap was right: They could have made another dumb flag! But now that he had chosen a path, he could not change direction. He was a leader. He had chosen the revenge path, and he would continue on that path, even if the way had grown tough. Even if there were very clear signs that read TURN BACK, THIS IS A BAD PATH. Even if there were roots and vines and stinging plants along the path, Josh Barkin would keep walking forward. In fact, he would run down that path, metaphorically, which in this metaphor meant that he would have *even bigger* revenge against the Terrible Two. Once he found them. If he found them. How would he find them?

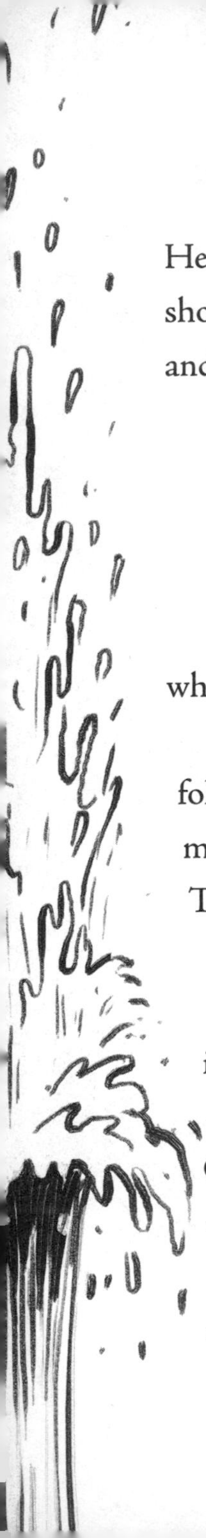

"Major Barkin! Major Barkin!"

Two familiar and identical voices came from behind Josh. He turned to see Mudflap and Splinters running along the shore, toward the dock. Josh drew himself up to his full height and stood where he was. Let them come to him.

"Major Barkin!"

"You're late."

"But sir!"

"LATE."

"Sir. We found one of them. The blond one. And we know where we can find him again."

They'd been out on RECON! Not planning a mutiny— following *his* orders, searching for *his* enemies. They loved him. They feared him. They respected him.

Josh smiled.

Then he tossed them both in the lake.

Over on land, a man with a buzz cut watched Josh toss Mudflap and Splinters off the dock. This man was the supreme commander. (Tim.) He held a clipboard, and the clipboard held a piece of paper. The paper said COUNSELOR EVALUATION: JOSH BARKIN. There were several categories: "YELLING," "PUSH-UPS," "PUT-DOWNS," "PUSHING AROUND," "TOSSING," and "GENERAL AGGRESSION." The supreme commander marked Josh "REALLY GREAT" in each category. ("REALLY GREAT" was the second-best category, right under "SUPREME.") He gave Josh a POWER RATING of 9 out of 10, which is the highest power rating he was willing to give. (Anything higher could be a threat to his own supremacy.) There was no doubt about it: Josh Barkin had real leadership potential. And the kid had only improved after the berating Tim had given him earlier that day, when he'd gotten stuck in that tree. Tim believed that sometimes a kid needed to get yelled at for a little while. It was a big part of why he had started Yawnee Valley Yelling and Push-Ups Camp. (The other part was Tim's belief that sometimes a kid needed to do a bunch of push-ups.) Tim felt a good berating built character. (What *kind* of character it built was something Tim didn't think too much about. Because of course you and I know that there is such a thing as a violent character. A nasty character. A bad character.)

Although he had never served in the military, Tim had seen a lot of army movies (and some navy movies as well), so he started a boot camp. Tim felt proud watching Josh yell and push. He felt he had been instrumental in developing Josh's character. Tim was a grown man who loved his job, which was to yell at children, and to teach them to yell at each other. What a world, what a world.

THREE DAYS LATER, Principal Barkin opened the front door of the Manzanita Cabin and was surprised to find a giant rock at his feet.

He frowned.

"I don't remember any of this," he said.

The "this" Principal Barkin referred to was the rock, which really was quite large, but also the message on the rock.

The rock was sitting there outside the cabin, right in his front yard. Well, "yard" wasn't quite the right word. Out here in nature, the whole world was his yard! Or at least the part of the world delineated as Yawnee Valley Regional Park and

Outdoor Recreational Area. But this was on the grassy bit beside his cabin, a slice of nature for which Principal Barkin felt especially responsible. Which made Principal Barkin wonder: Should he turn this rock over?

He unzipped his Principal Pack, which most people call a fanny pack, but Principal Barkin called a Principal Pack, even in the summer, and pulled out a pencil and paper.

SHOULD I TURN THIS ROCK OVER?

REASONS WHY, YES, I SHOULD TURN THIS ROCK OVER:

1. Talking rock!
2. It is in my "yard."
3. Might be treasure underneath.
4. Might be entrance to an underground world underneath.
5. Park Rangers might think I wrote on the rock and arrest me.
6. WHAT IS UNDER THAT ROCK????

REASONS WHY, NO, I SHOULD NOT TURN THIS ROCK OVER:
1. The rock looks really heavy.
2. This feels like a prank.

Principal Barkin chewed on his pencil eraser. There was no doubt about it: This was a stumper. He would think about his options on his morning hike. The fresh air and solitude would help him come to a careful decision.

Principal Barkin set off on the trail.

Then he turned around and came right back to the rock.

"CONFOUND YOU, ROCK!" he shouted at the rock.

On the one hand, this was almost definitely a prank. Those two rogues, Miles and Niles, were running loose in these woods, pranking willy-nilly. Principal Barkin had a good idea of what it felt like to be pranked by Niles Sparks and Miles Murphy, the sickening sensation of the world very slowly, then very suddenly, turning upside down. He felt it in his stomach, like riding on a roller coaster.

On the other hand, what was under that rock????????

It was very strange. Very interesting. Exciting, even. Which is why it must be a prank! An ordinary day suddenly taking a left turn into absurdity. Cars parked on top of steps. Flowers spelling out rude nonsense. Rocks talking. Well, not talking, exactly. But sort of talking. "Turn me over." "Turn ME over." Who would be so audacious as to speak for a rock? I mean, really! Who would be so bizarre? A pair of pranksters like Miles and Niles, that's who!

Yes! It was definitely a prank.

Principal Barkin set off on the trail again.

Then he turned around and came right back to the rock. Again.

Even if it was a prank (and it was almost certainly a prank), WHAT WAS UNDER THAT ROCK????????

Principal Barkin was curious. I mean, how could he not be curious? Of course, curiosity killed the cat. But Principal Barkin was not a cat. Principal Barkin was a principal.

What would his father, Former Principal Bertrand Barkin, say? He would say something like, "UNDER NO CIRCUMSTANCES SHOULD YOU FALL VICTIM TO A PRANK, BARRY! REPORT THOSE TWO VANDALS TO THE AUTHORITIES AT ONCE! THEN LEAVE THE FOREST, WHICH IS A RIDICULOUS PLACE TO BE, AND GO SOMEPLACE YOU BELONG, LIKE A SUMMER TEACHER TRAINING IN-SERVICE.

IT IS WHAT I WOULD DO. IT IS WHAT YOUR BROTHER, BOB BARKIN, WHOM I HAVE ALWAYS LIKED BETTER, WOULD DO, IF HE WERE A PRINCIPAL AND NOT A SUCCESSFUL DAIRY FARMER. STOP STANDING THERE BY THE ROCK! YOU ARE BEING FRIVOLOUS. GIVE JOSH AND SHARON MY LOVE."

What would his son, Future Principal Josh Barkin, say? That was harder for Principal Barkin to predict, but it would probably involve calling him a nimbus.

For the last time, Principal Barkin set off on the trail.

And for the last time, he turned around and came back to the rock.

Because:

Even if it was a prank,

what was under that rock????????

And also:

Even if it was a prank,

was it really so bad to get pranked?

He would turn the rock over.

"OK, MILES AND NILES!" Principal Barkin shouted to the trees all around him. "I KNOW YOU ARE PROBABLY WATCHING ME, AND PRANKING ME. WHAT I DO

NEXT, I DO IN FULL KNOWLEDGE OF WHAT IS PROBABLY GOING ON RIGHT NOW.

"JUST SO YOU KNOW," he added.

"OK," he said. "I'M GOING TO TURN OVER THE ROCK."

The rock was really heavy.

But Principal Barkin, having decided to turn over the rock, and now having announced his intentions, was determined.

He tried to pry the rock loose with his walking stick,

which snapped.

"GOOD-BYE, STICK!" said Principal Barkin. "THANK YOU FOR YOUR SERVICE!"

Principal Barkin tried every which way to turn over that rock.

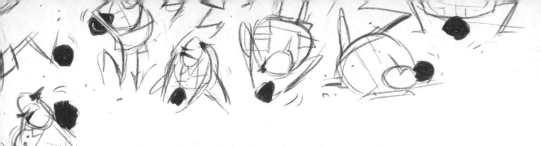

Until finally he found a way that worked.

"HERE WE GO!" said Principal Barkin. "GENTLY NOW! GENTLY! AHA! HA HA HA! AH!"

The rock tipped over and turned upside down.

"Oh," said Principal Barkin.

"Oh boy," he added.

The other side of the rock also had a message.

THANKS! NOW TURN ME BACK OVER SO I CAN PRANK SOMEBODY ELSE

"AH!" Principal Barkin shouted. "HA HA!" (He actually shouted "HA HA!")

Principal Barkin smiled.

Then he stopped smiling.

He flushed.

Principal Barkin's face turned the shade of a late-summer plum.

It was one thing to be pranked.

But if Principal Barkin turned this rock back over, wouldn't he *become a prankster?*

This was cause for fretting. And so Principal Barkin began to fret.

"Two roads are diverging in a . . . *green* wood," said Principal Barkin, approximately quoting a beloved American poem.

"And one is the path I have traveled my whole life," he continued, taking some artistic liberties with the poem.

"And then there is another path, a pranking path, and *that* is a pretty major difference," he said, really butchering the poem at this point.

A pranking principal. Who could imagine such a thing? Sure, Principal Barkin had participated in one prank, a prank on his father, a prank that made him chuckle even now, when he thought about it. But he had not been a principal at the time—he'd been on an involuntary, indefinite leave of absence. But of course that prank had led to his reinstatement to his proper place as principal, and so this was a whole different matter. A pranking principal. It was silly. No. It was beyond silly. It was absolutely ridiculous.

However, it did have a nice ring to it. Pranking principal. Both words beginning with the same letter. Just like the Terrible Two! He could have his own secret club, a rival secret club, the Pranking Principals! Although who else would join? Certainly not his father, who would probably say something like, "'PRANKING PRINCIPAL' IS AN INHERENT CONTRADICTION, LIKE 'LAZY SUNDAY' OR 'INNOCENT JOKE.' I AM AGHAST THAT YOU WOULD EVEN CONSIDER TURNING THAT ROCK OVER, BARRY. THIS SITUATION IS EXACTLY WHY I TOLD YOU TO NEVER GO TO THE WOODS, AS WELL AS SEVERAL OTHER REASONS. YOU DISAPPOINT ME, UNLIKE YOUR BROTHER, BOB, WHO IS SERIOUS IN ALL THAT HE DOES, INCLUDING HIS BUSINESS MILKING COWS AND SELLING THAT MILK TO GROCERY STORES. HE WOULD HAVE MADE A VERY FINE PRINCIPAL.

BUT YOU, BARRY? WHAT SORT OF BARKIN ARE YOU?"

Thinking of his father made Principal Barkin turn an even darker purple, the shade of the blackberries that grew in the brambles by Miles and Niles's little green glade. And like an overripe blackberry, Principal Barkin looked like he might just burst.

He burst out laughing instead.

And then Principal Barkin set to turning the rock back over.

(The rock was still really heavy.)

"There," he said, and patted the rock on what would have been its head, if rocks had heads, which of course they don't.

The rock was back just the way it had been before.

But Principal Barkin felt like a different principal.

"WOW," SAID NILES, watching his principal pat the rock into place. "I kind of didn't think he would actually do it."

Miles agreed. "I thought maybe we were going to break his brain."

They were standing in a thick grove a few yards from the Manzanita Cabin, obscured by greenery from a principal's peering eyes. Miles and Niles exchanged a secret high five, the Roman numeral high five, or high two.

Then they presented themselves to their principal and gave him a high five (just a regular high five).

Principal Barkin was delighted to see them.

"Well, well, well," he said. "If it isn't the Terrible Two."

"The Terrible *Two*," said Miles.

"I said that," said Principal Barkin.

Miles replayed it in his brain. "Oh. So you did. Wow."

"Well, boys," said Principal Barkin, "it looks like I've joined your club."

"We're not doing the Terrible Three thing," said Miles.

"Oh. No. I meant the larger club. The worldwide confederation of pranksters."

"The International Order of Disorder," said Niles.

"Oh. Is that what it's called? Neat. In any case, I am of your ilk. Who knows what adventures are in store for us?" He checked his watch. "For example, it is half past eleven, so I can still go on my morning hike. Would you care to join me?"

"Um," said Miles. "No thank you."

"I see," said Principal Barkin. "Well. I could always make it an afternoon hike, if you would care to join me for a morning hot chocolate?"

Miles *did* like hot chocolate. And Principal Barkin *did* seem like he needed the company.

"Sure!" said Miles.

Niles checked his own watch.

"Actually," he said, "I can't. But you two have fun."

Miles gave Niles a look like, *Dude. Are you kidding me?*

Niles gave Miles a look like, *Sorry! I have to go.*

Miles gave Niles a look like, *You're just going to leave me here with Principal Barkin?*

Meanwhile, Principal Barkin was also giving Niles a look, one like, *You're just going to leave me here with Miles Murphy?*

But Niles didn't know Principal Barkin well enough to interpret his looks.

Niles said good-bye. Miles and Principal Barkin watched him go.

"Well, Miles," said Principal Barkin, "the good news is the cabin only has two mugs, so now you won't have to drink out of a cereal bowl."

PRINCIPAL BARKIN EMPTIED two packets of hot chocolate mix into the mugs and poured hot water from a kettle. Miles fished a dehydrated marshmallow out of his mug, so he could crunch on it before it got soft.

"So," said Principal Barkin.

"So," said Miles.

They each took a sip.

"Ooh. Hot!" said Principal Barkin.

"Yeah," said Miles.

Principal Barkin blew on his hot chocolate.

So did Miles.

Miles was reminded of the many other times he'd sat across from Principal Barkin—usually in Principal Barkin's office, in a low chair on the wrong side of Principal Barkin's desk, while Principal Barkin turned purple and shouted at him.

This was different. It was almost . . . pleasant.

(Only almost, though.)

Principal Barkin was reminded of the many times he'd sat at this same table, in this same cabin, with a completely different kid: his son, Josh Barkin. He and Josh would sit drinking the same hot chocolate (different packets, of course, but from the same giant box that had been in the cabin's pantry for years), listening to the same birds chirping (different individual birds, presumably, but probably from the same general assortment of species—Principal Barkin didn't know much about birds), while inside the cabin Josh sat silently— just as Miles sat silently right now. This silence, though, Miles's silence, was a different kind of silence. Josh's silence was more of a sullen silence, or sometimes an exasperated silence. Often it was a disappointed silence, very much like the silence that accompanied the withering paternal glances of Barry Barkin's father, Former Principal Bertrand Barkin. (There was no doubt about it: The boy resembled his grandfather. Remarkable what skips a generation.) Josh's silence was like a force field, inside of which Josh slouched and sighed (silently).

The silence that had descended on the table he shared with Miles was different. For one thing, Miles was not rolling his eyes or staring at the knots in the cabin's wood walls. Miles was looking at him, smiling. This silence was a chasm across which Miles was reaching. Principal Barkin got the sense that Miles would prefer this silence be broken—and that it was Principal Barkin's job to break it. And so break it he would! Principal Barkin cast about for some suitable topic of conversation.

It took him a long time to think of something.

Even longer.

Aha!

"Miles," said Principal Barkin, "I've always wanted to ask what happened to your dad, but I was afraid it would make things uncomfortable."

Miles nodded.

Principal Barkin coughed.

There was some more silence.

"Did I just make things uncomfortable?"

"Yeah."

"Oh."

Silence.

"Well," said Principal Barkin, "in any case, I bring this up because I was thinking. And what I was thinking was, maybe I can be a sort of father figure to you. Do you ever see me that way? As a role model?"

"Honestly? Not really."

"Ah."

"I guess Niles is kind of my role model," said Miles.

"Yes," said Principal Barkin, "mine too. Well, I suppose I am simply your principal. And that's good enough for me."

Miles sipped his hot chocolate.

"Maybe we could be friends," said Miles.

"Oh!"

Principal Barkin smiled.

Then Principal Barkin frowned.

"Well, that's not very good at all."

"Why not?" Miles asked.

"Miles," said Principal Barkin, "a principal stands atop the pinnacle of power. There is no room at the tip of that spire for anybody but the principal. And so I must stand alone, or risk losing my balance, the balance of power, and fall into the abyss, which in this metaphor is a school where food fights happen every day, or something like that . . ." Principal Barkin had fallen into the abyss of his own metaphor. "Anyway, a principal cannot be friends with students. Or faculty. Or staff."

"But what about that expression?" Miles asked. "You know, 'The principal is your pal.'"

"That's just an expression," said Principal Barkin, "to help you remember how to spell 'principal.' I prefer the following mnemonic: 'A principal can never be your pal.' Same end result, and it's truer. Of course, the best way to remember how to spell 'principal' is to drill it into your brain by writing it over and over again several hundred times on many sheets of binder paper."

Miles shrugged. "OK."

There was some more silence.

"It was a very nice sentiment, Miles!" said Principal Barkin. "But soon summer will be over. We will leave this forest and enter our school. I must maintain my authority."

"Appealing to your authority is the weakest way to be powerful."

"Who said that? Was that me or Sun Tzu?"

"It's something Niles says sometimes."

"Ah. Interesting kid."

"Yeah."

Principal Barkin set down his mug.

"What does it mean?"

"I have no idea."

"Well," said Principal Barkin, "it's certainly something to think about."

"Yeah."

Sitting, thinking, drinking hot chocolate, they settled into a pleasant silence.

NILES, MEANWHILE, was experiencing an unpleasant silence. He had arrived ten minutes early to his rendezvous with Holly, picked out a good sitting rock, and started reading. Niles was almost finished with his book, which was very funny but also very sad.

But Niles couldn't concentrate.

Something was amiss.

It was the silence. You would think it would be easy to read when it's quiet, but something tickled something at the edge of Niles's brain. This was an eerie silence. A foreboding silence.

Niles stared at his feet, which looked extra pale in the water, especially the parts normally covered by his socks.

He closed his eyes and tried to calm his brain down. He could feel the warm sun on the outside of his eyelids. It was nice.

Niles tried his book again. He was on the last chapter. A king was remembering all the animals a wizard had turned him into when he was a boy who lived in the woods: a falcon, a badger, a fish, an ant, a goose.

The goose!

That's what was odd: The goose was not at the swimming hole. Normally the big gray goose would be honking at Niles, and lunging at Niles, and trying to bite Niles. But the gray goose was gone, and the place wasn't the same without him. Niles wondered where he'd gone. Maybe he'd left—it was late in the summer—and was heading south, someplace warmer. Niles smiled, imagining how it would be to fly among a flock of geese.

Still, it seemed early to migrate. It was only mid-August, and today was plenty warm. Niles made a note to do some

research on geese that night, when he got back to his house. When Niles came across something he didn't know, he liked to know it as soon as he could.

Satisfied that he'd solved one mystery, and excited he'd soon solve another, Niles checked his watch. Holly should be getting here soon. He picked up his book.

Niles heard footsteps behind him but didn't look up. He wanted to get to the end of his sentence.

"Hey, Holly," he said, looking down at the page.

"Hi, nimbus," said Josh, looking down at Niles.

Then two pairs of identical arms held Niles down while Josh pulled a pillowcase over his head. Papa Company carried Niles off into the forest.

MILES MURPHY was worried.
You could see it on his face.

"Worry"
(*n. concern, unease*)

For the last hour, he'd been trying not to worry. It was 4:00 P.M. Niles had been gone since before noon. And sure, it was normal for Niles to disappear, but all summer Niles had never been gone for more than three hours. Three hours was an hour ago. That's when Miles had started to feel weird. But he'd told himself that Niles was capable, Niles was smart. Niles was clever and took care of himself. At 3:00 on the dot, Miles had wanted to run through the forest screaming Niles's name. But

Miles decided he was overreacting. He decided to wait. He'd stay at the cave. He'd give Niles an hour. He'd wait until 4:00, and then he'd get worried.

For an hour Miles sat there, watching his watch.

Now it was 4:00.

Miles Murphy was worried.

He ran through the forest, screaming Niles's name.

"Niles!" said Miles.

"Niles!" said Miles.

"Niles! Niles! Niles!" said Miles.

He checked Principal Barkin's cabin. Empty. He checked back at their cave. Empty. He checked all the places he and Niles liked to go: the big stump, the haunted gully, the spigot where people gave their dogs drinks. Niles was nowhere.

"Niles!" said Miles.

"Hey, Johnny," said Holly. Miles almost ran into her on the trail that ran by the archery fields. "You looking for the Great Gondorff?"

"What?" said Miles. "Oh! That's from a movie!"

Holly looked surprised.

"I know," said Holly. "How did *you* know?"

"Niles made me watch it the other night. Well, not *made*

me. At first I didn't want to, because it seemed pretty old, but actually it was really good!"

"Yeah," said Holly.

"We watched another one with those same guys. Where they were cowboys. I don't know where Niles finds out about these things. You look kind of surprised!"

(It's true: Holly still looked surprised.)

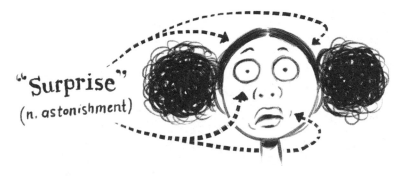

"Surprise"
(n. astonishment)

(She'd been telling people about movies for years.)

(But nobody ever actually *watched* them.)

"OK," said Miles. "I gotta go. I'm looking for Niles!"

"Me too," said Holly. "He stood me up."

"What?"

"We were supposed to meet at noon today."

"You were?"

"Yeah. We've been hanging out all summer, over at the swimming hole."

"The one with the goose?"

"Yeah. Niles didn't tell you?"

"No." So this was Niles's secret? Miles wondered why Niles hadn't told him.

"OH." Miles figured out why Niles hadn't told him. "Huh."

Holly frowned. "I waited around for him all afternoon. He must have left before I got there."

"What do you mean?"

"He left his book."

Holly handed Miles a book with a sword on its cover.

"Will you give this back to him when you see him?"

Niles would never forget his book.

Miles ran off without saying good-bye.

PAPA COMPANY HAD TAKEN Niles back to their barracks, tied him up with some rope, and gone to eat dinner. (Even villains have to eat dinner.)

"We'll be back, nimbus," Josh said when the dinner bugle sounded.

"Yeah, nimbus," said Mudflap.

Josh glared at Mudflap.

Then the three of them left Niles alone.

Niles heard them block the door to the cabin with something heavy.

Then he heard Josh say, "Don't say nimbus. That's my word."

After that, he could hear only the blood pumping around in his own head.

"Let's see," said Niles. He worked at the knots that held his hands behind his back. The ropes were tied tight. His wrists hurt. Niles had to give Josh credit for one thing: He was good at knots.

He went to the door, turned the knob with his hands

(which was tricky with his back turned), and threw his weight into opening it.

That didn't work either.

(Niles didn't weigh much.)

He considered jumping through the window, but that seemed unwise. Plus the window was up pretty high.

(Niles wasn't good at jumping.)

Niles sat on the floor.

This was bad.

He closed his eyes and thought.

There was a chattering outside, and the sound of tapping on glass. Niles opened his eyes and saw a squirrel standing on the other side of a window. It stood on the sill, eating a nut. This squirrel looked familiar. It's hard to tell squirrels apart, but this squirrel looked a lot like the one they had freed.

See? Now flip to page 41 and compare the two squirrels.

It *was* the same squirrel!

"Hey, squirrel," said Niles. "Looks like the tables have turned."

This was quite a coincidence. It felt fated to be. Now the squirrel could squeeze through a hole in the wall. It could chew through Niles's bonds and free up his hands. Niles could open the window and climb out to freedom. The squirrel would follow a ways into the woods. "Thanks, squirrel," Niles would say, and the squirrel would chirp back. Then they'd part ways. They'd be even, the squirrel's debt repaid.

But none of that happened.

(This isn't that kind of book.)

The squirrel finished its nut and scampered away.

Niles examined his situation. He ran through his options. He plotted and schemed. But escape seemed impossible, at least for the time being. So there was only one thing to do: Wait.

Still, Niles wasn't one to just sit around.

Walking backward, his arms out, Niles began to explore.

Sure, it looked a bit silly,

but who could say what he'd find?

Well, here's what he found:

Under the mattresses of various cots, Niles found candy bars, cookies, and three comic books (all of these things were forbidden at camp). In a pillowcase he found letters from one camper's mom. He put all this stuff back and remade the beds, tucking the green blankets tight, with hospital corners.

Under each cot was a duffel bag. Each bag was drab green. One of the bags bore a name, spelled out in block letters: JOSH BARKIN.

This was something Niles was quite glad to find.

He opened the bag and found more things inside. Shirts, shorts, long pants. Sunglasses. Bug spray. A stack of envelopes, stamped, addressed to "Dad," in Principal Barkin's hand. Socks. Flip-flops. Sunscreen. A "Future Principal Pack" (a fanny pack that said "Future Principal Josh Barkin, from Dad" written in Sharpie). A shampoo bottle (still full). A comb. Two washcloths, both damp. A flashlight. A hacky sack. A bag full of batteries. Six carefully folded—oh. Oh my. Well, this was interesting. At the bottom of the bag, below a blue towel, Niles found—

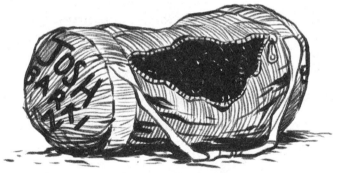

The door to the cabin flew open.

Someone stood silhouetted by the late-afternoon sun.

"Niles!" said Miles.

"Miles!" said Niles.

Niles held out two fingers for a behind-the-back handshake.

Miles took some time to untie his friend.

(One thing about Miles: He was not great at knots.)

"I knew you'd come," Niles said.

"How?" Miles asked.

Niles shrugged. "I just knew."

"Oh come on!" Miles said. "Don't tell me getting kidnapped was just some genius scheme you've been cooking up!" Miles rolled his eyes. He'd been feeling so proud. He'd leapt into action. He'd saved the day. Saved the summer! Saved his best friend! As soon as Holly handed Miles that book, he'd guessed what had happened. He'd guessed—and guessed right! Had a hunch! Acted on it! He'd hightailed it to the camp. Snuck past barbed wire. Crawled around on his belly. Crept by the mess hall. Miles had hidden behind the tires of a giant Humvee. He'd checked nine different cabins. Found Niles. Freed Niles. Untied all these knots. Knots were tricky! But he'd done it. Untied seventeen knots! And now it would be like he'd done none of these things. It would be like Niles did it: his brain, Miles's body. Now Niles would say it was his plan all along.

"Of course not!" Niles said. "Josh had me beat! He and those stooges snuck up on me. They pulled a pillowcase over my head!"

"They what?" Miles said.

"Yeah!" Niles replied. "I probably should have known, looking back on it now."

Now Niles was looking down at the floor.

"That goose didn't migrate. Those jerks probably scared him away."

(Niles was right. They'd thrown rocks at him, after the goose had tried to bite Josh.)

"I couldn't figure out any way to escape from this cabin. There were only two ways this could end. Josh would win. Or you'd save me. And even though I couldn't figure out how you would do it, the latter seemed more likely. I just had a feeling.

I don't know why. But I did. So I waited. I knew you would come for me. And then you did."

(That's the kind of book this is: a book about friends.)

Miles smiled.

"Oh," said Miles.

"Yeah," said Niles. "So. Thanks!"

"Sure," said Miles. He nodded toward the door. "Well. Let's go."

Miles made for the exit.

Niles followed.

Then he stopped.

"Still," said Niles, "all that being said. Now that we're both here, it doesn't feel right to just sneak out the front door."

Miles turned around slowly.

"What?" Miles asked.

"I mean, what kind of message does that send to Josh?"

Miles knew the look on his friend's face. "You've got some genius scheme."

"I don't know about genius."

"Uh-huh," Miles said. He couldn't believe they were talking, not running back to the woods. But when he heard Niles's plan, it *did* sound pretty good.

Miles nodded.

Niles smiled.

"OK," Niles said. He faced toward the wall and held out his hands. "Tie me back up!"

Miles sighed.

Great.

More knots.

JOSH BARKIN KICKED THE DOOR OPEN for dramatic effect.

"WE'RE BACK, NIMBUS!" he PLOPped.

"Yeah, *nombus*," said Mudflap. "Look out! We're back!"

Josh punched Mudflap's arm. "Nombus?" he asked.

"Like nimbus, but different."

They would revisit this later. Josh didn't want to show disunity in front of the prisoner. Besides, Papa Company didn't have much time. They had the barracks to themselves, but just till lights out, at 2030. Two hours: 120 mikes to get this nimbus to talk.

Niles was sitting on a cot. Josh plopped (lowercase plopped) down next to him. He put a friendly arm around Niles's shoulders. He flashed Niles his friendliest grin.

If you walked into the cabin at that moment, with no idea what was going on, you might think that two good friends were having a pleasant conversation, except that one of them was tied up with ropes.

"Niles, let's talk. I think we can both agree that our prank war, which was started in such a funny way when you captured our flag"—Josh squeezed Niles's shoulder very hard—"has now just gotten absolutely out of hand. I mean, look at you! You're tied up with lots of great knots, captured and stashed in an enemy camp! That's crazy! How did this even happen? It's just nuts. So I say, for your sake, but also mine, for all our sakes, let's just end it. You know? Let's just call this over, chalk it up as another Josh Barkin victory. Tell me where you're hiding our flag, and I'll let you off easy. I'll untie you and set you free, after I punch you in the leg or something. Something minor like that. OK?"

Niles considered Josh's offer.

"No thanks, nombus."

Mudflap stifled a laugh, but he didn't stifle it very well.

"Mudflap was laughing at this funny joke I made earlier, at dinner," Josh said, "not because you said nombus. Right, Mudflap?"

"Yes, sir," said Mudflap.

"OK," said Niles.

"I'm serious," said Josh.

"OK," said Niles.

The prisoner had declined Josh's offer. Josh had figured he would. But Mudflap had disrupted the rhythm of the interrogation. They were supposed to be running an enhanced version of the old Good Cop–Bad Cop technique, a variation Josh had invented himself: the Powerful Cop–Silently Loyal Cop–Identical Silently Loyal Cop technique. Splinters was doing a great job. Josh decided that Mudflap was definitely his least favorite cadet.

Josh stood up and stomped, attempting to reestablish the menacing atmosphere that had dissipated somewhat with the nombus episode. "Fine! If you refuse to talk, then we'll *prank* the information out of you!"

Niles winced.

"Well, Splinters, where should we begin?"

Splinters, who'd spent the last ten mikes trying his best to be silently loyal, was confused: Should he answer Major Barkin's question, which would be loyal, or just stand there, which was silent?

"Why are you making that weird face?" Josh asked.

(It's true: Splinters was grimacing under the stress of his decision.)

"JUST ANSWER THE QUESTION!" Josh PLOPped.

"Um," said Splinters, "we could cut his hair?"

The camp had several pairs of clippers that were used to give the cadets buzz cuts.

"Interesting," said Josh. He mulled the proposal in a manner he felt was menacing. "No. It'd probably be an improvement. He needs a haircut."

"What?" said Niles.

"Mudflap, how about you? Any ideas?"

"That's what I was going to say too," Mudflap said. "Same thing as my brother."

"What's the point of there being two of you if you just think of all the same stuff?" Josh shook his head. "Twins."

(Mudflap's answer had nothing to do with Splinters being his twin. Mudflap just hadn't heard Josh's question, or Splinters's answer, because he was still thinking of nombuses.)

"Well," said Josh, "I have a better idea. We'll make him swallow rocks."

Niles slumped.

Two years ago—two years ago to the day, actually (it was quite a coincidence!)—Josh Barkin had found Niles reading upside down on some monkey bars in the park. He'd pulled him down onto the tanbark and forced him to swallow a pebble. Then a week later, Josh had tracked Niles down and made him do it again, this time with a slightly bigger rock. Careful readers of this series may remember that these episodes are part of what got Niles interested in pranking to begin with.

"Mudflap, Splinters, go fetch a bunch of rocks. I'll stay here and guard the prisoner."

Niles hoped Miles made it back to the cabin before the rocks did.

PAST BIRCH AND DOGWOOD and incense cedar, past buckthorn and hemlock, cherry and sweet gum, past chestnut, past locust, past willow, past yew, past ash and basswood, past walnut and holly, past pine, past oak, past hickory, Miles Murphy sprinted through the woods.

NILES STARED at a plate full of rocks.

The plate was on a chair next to his cot.

He noticed that all three classifications of rock were represented there—igneous, sedimentary, and metamorphic—which is the kind of thing he'd find neat, if he wasn't going to have to eat them.

Josh squatted down so that his face loomed behind the rocks. He thought it would make a menacing picture.

(He wasn't wrong.)

"Last chance, nimbus," said Josh. "Tell me where you stashed our flag, and I'll let you go."

Niles looked toward the door of the cabin.

Josh laughed.

"Think your friend is going to come in and save you, nimbus? He's not. And even if he showed up, we'd have you outnumbered, three to two. We're bigger than you two. We're stronger than you two. Plus there's not even two of you right now, so we've really got you beat. Hey: the Terrible One! That's a pretty good joke!"

(It was not a good joke.)

Josh picked up a rock.

(A bit of slate, a metamorphic rock formed from shale, a sedimentary rock.)

"Mudflap, Splinters, hold him down."

The twins moved toward Niles, Mudflap on the left, Splinters on the right.

But before they could reach him, Niles did something strange.

He leaned forward toward the plate, and, using only his lips (remember: His hands were tied behind his back), he picked up a rock.

Then Niles straightened his back.

He looked Josh right in the eye.

And Niles smiled.

Grinned, really.

Grinned, holding the rock right between his front teeth.

What Niles did next was stranger.

He swallowed the rock.

"AHHHHHHHHHHHHHHHHHHHHHHHHH-HHH!" said Mudflap.

"OHHHHHHHHHHHHHHHHHHHHHHHHH-HHH!" said Splinters.

Josh didn't say anything.

Niles nodded appreciatively and said, "Delicious."

"THAT IS SO SO GROSS!" said Mudflap.

"HE *LIKES* IT!" said Splinters.

"IT'S THE GROSSEST THING I'VE EVER SEEN," said Mudflap. (He thought, but didn't say, AND MAYBE ALSO THE COOLEST.)

Niles could feel where the rock had traveled down his esophagus. There was still grit in his mouth. The rock sat in his belly. The rock was not delicious. It was awful. But Niles still smiled. He hoped that if he ate one rock, maybe he wouldn't be forced to eat them all.

(He wasn't wrong.)

Josh threw the plate against the wall. It smashed, scattering shards and rocks across the barracks' pine floors.

"OK, this freak is weird. Mudflap, clean up the plate and the rocks. Splinters, go get the clippers. We'll shave off his hair."

T HE SUN WAS SETTING when Miles kicked open the door to the Why-Pees' cabin.

He hoped he wasn't too late.

"Oh," Miles said.

Here's what he saw:

It looked like he was a little late.

"Wow," said Miles. "Sorry."

"Took you long enough," said Niles.

"I had to run all the way to the cave!" said Miles.

"Ha ha!" said Josh. (He actually said "Ha ha!") "A cave! So you guys have a cave. Probably where you're keeping my flag!"

"Our flag," said Mudflap.

"Our flag," said Josh. "Tell me where your cave is! Or I'll shave the rest of your little friend's hair off!"

"Now that you've started," said Niles, "I'd actually prefer it if you shaved the rest of my hair off."

"Well," said Josh. "Then tell me where your cave is or I *won't* shave the rest of your little friend's hair off!"

Josh brandished the clippers above his head, sort of menacingly.

"Dude," said Miles. "I *brought* your flag. Just let him go."

Miles took off his backpack and took out Papa Company's flag.

Josh smiled. "A prisoner swap?"

"I guess," Miles said.

"Man, why do you care about your flag so much?"

"It's not the flag, nimbus. It's *winning*. You thought you could take something from me. But you can't. I'm better than you. Stronger than you. Smarter than you. The flag is a symbol. Of winning. I won the prank war."

"We won the prank war," said Splinters.

"We won the prank war," said Josh. "Under my leadership. I won. You lost."

"Josh," Miles said, "this isn't a prank war. You're not a prankster. You're a jerk. You tell someone to walk up close to you, just so you can throw a stick at his head?"

(Splinters was surprised and embarrassed to know Miles had seen that.)

"That's not a prank," said Miles. "A prank *says* something. What does throwing sticks say?"

"It says I'm in charge," Josh said.

"Pranks do not belong to the powerful! The prank is too fine an instrument for a brute's clumsy fingers!"

Niles smiled.

"The prank belongs to the powerless! It is the mustache across the dictator's portrait, the tweak of the tyrant's nose!"

Niles smiled even more.

"What have you added to the sum total of human joy?"

Miles asked. "Nothing! You just make people miserable! That's not a prank. That's being a jerk. You're not a prankster. You're a jerk, Josh Barkin. A bully. Which is why you get pranked. That's what happens to jerks. You don't know when to stop. But I do. This is over."

He placed the flag down on a cot.

"So you're saying you surrender," said Josh.

"Yeah, fine. I surrender."

"And you, little nimbus?"

"Sure, Josh," said Niles. "I surrender."

"See that, cadets? That's how you win. Untie that dork."

The twins undid Niles's ropes.

Niles stood up.

"Wait, nimbus," said Josh.

He punched Niles in the leg. "I won!"

"Great, Josh," said Niles.

He limped out the door.

Miles left too.

The Terrible Two walked up a hill that sat outside the camp.

"Nice speech," Niles said.

"Most of it was just stuff I stole from you," Miles said.

"Not that last bit," said Niles. "And that was the best part."

"I don't think any of it sunk in."

"Yeah," said Niles. "It was still worth trying. But I don't think speeches ever really do much to change people's minds. Especially people like Josh."

The sun was down, but the sky was still bright. They sat on the hilltop, in a patch of damp grass.

"Oh," said Miles. "I have something for you."

He reached into his backpack and took out Niles's book.

"Where'd you find that?" Niles asked.

"I ran into Holly," said Miles. "She wanted me to return it."

"Ah," said Niles. He took his book back. "OK."

In the twilight, Miles could see that his friend was blushing.

"It's cool, man," Miles said.

"Ha ha," Niles said.

For a while Miles didn't say anything, and Niles didn't say anything.

For the rest of his life, Niles would remember what this moment sounded like—the noise of the forest coming to life at dusk, and the silence of two best friends sitting on a hill.

The summer Niles spent in these woods was a summer he didn't have to decide who he'd be at school, or who he'd be at home, a perfect summer where Niles could just be Niles—whoever that was. Niles wasn't sure he knew. But Miles seemed to. When Niles was with Miles, he never had to decide who he would be. In that way, spending time with Miles was like spending time in the woods. And so spending time in the woods with Miles was the best time of all. Niles smiled at the passing thought.

"Hey." Miles elbowed his friend in the ribs. "It's starting."

JOSH BARKIN HAD A REALLY GOOD IDEA. His
good idea was this: a really cool way to celebrate his recent
victory over a couple of dumb nimbuses. And that really cool
way was—

"A parade!" Mudflap said. "We should have a parade!"

"We're not having a parade," Josh said. "This will be even
better."

There was a tall flagpole at the center of camp. There, the
American flag was hoisted at sunrise and taken down at sunset. So now the flagpole was empty, but there was still plenty
of light.

"Come on," said Josh. "Hurry up, grab the flag."

Papa Company gathered at the base of the flagpole.

"Raise it high," Josh said.

This would be Papa Company's finest hour.

"Won't we get in trouble?" Mudflap asked.

"Can a flag even fly after sunset?" asked Splinters.

"THAT'S AN ORDER!" Josh PLOPped.

The twins unfolded the flag. Mudflap fastened it to the rope. Splinters worked the pulley. A fair breeze unfurled the flag against a purple sky. Papa Company's insignia flew high for all to admire: a white rattlesnake skeleton on a field of pure black.

Wait.

Oh boy.

That was white.

But it wasn't a skeleton.

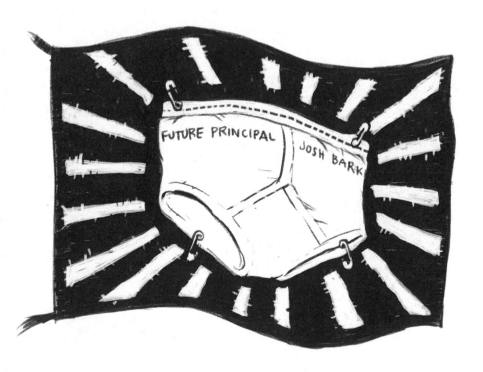

"PULL IT DOWN!" Josh PLOPped.

"Oh my gosh," Mudflap said.

"PULL IT DOWN!"

"Whose *are* those?" Splinters asked.

"I SAID PULL IT DOWN!"

"They're Josh's!" said Mudflap.

"They say his name on them!" said Splinters.

"How'd they get on there?" said Mudflap.

Then he started to laugh.

(Once he started laughing, Mudflap didn't much care how they got on there. But Miles had put them there, of course, after Niles had found them at the bottom of Josh's duffel bag.)

"THAT'S AN ORDER!" PLOPped Josh.

Mudflap and Splinters did not follow Josh's order.

They just laughed. The twins laughed so hard they dropped to the ground.

The commotion attracted the attention of some cadets marching nearby, who altered their route and stared up at the flag.

Scotty laughed.

Jackson laughed.

Darius laughed. (Laughing made him forget how much marching hurt his knees.)

Josh was as purple as a sunset in summer, a sunset that gave off enough light to clearly read Josh's name on his drawers.

"COMPANY, LEAVE!" Josh PLOPped. "THAT IS AN ORDER!"

Nobody left.

Mudflap stood up.

"New order!" said Mudflap. "Major Barkin's underwear salute!"

"I give the orders!" said Josh.

"Hey, that's an acronym!" said Splinters.

"I make the acronyms!" said Josh.

Josh ran through the words again in his head. New Order: Major Barkin's Underwear Salute.

"NOMBUS!" said Splinters, and he saluted the flag.

Mudflap fell back on the ground, saluting the flag.

All the cadets saluted the flag.

"Stop that!" said Josh. "Stop saluting!"

Nobody stopped saluting.

This was a crisis. Josh Barkin's command had come under threat. He felt his power slipping away. Josh desperately needed to reestablish control. What could he do? What would his father do? He would turn purple and embarrass himself.

What would his grandfather do? He would act, not react. Josh would be like his grandfather.

Josh Barkin drew himself up to his full height, which was tall.

He summoned his full voice, which was loud.

He arranged his face into an expression that was serious and stern.

Then he said: "Mudflap! Splinters! Pull down my shorts!"

In that moment, the cadets' laughter ceased.

"Sir?" said Mudflap.

"PULL DOWN MY SHORTS!" shouted Josh. "THAT IS AN ORDER!"

Mudflap looked at Splinters.

Splinters looked at Mudflap.

They smiled and shrugged, and then they pulled down Josh's shorts.

It was a full-blown mutiny.

CAREFUL STUDENTS OF THE HISTORY of the Barkin family may remember that something very similar had happened to Josh's grandfather, Bertrand Barkin, and when he had been the very same age. Niles, still sitting on the hilltop, smiled at the symmetry. Remarkable what skips a generation.

"Well," said Miles. (He was sitting on the hilltop too, of course.) "That was unexpected."

"What was unexpected?" Niles asked.

"He pranked himself."

"Oh," said Niles, "I think you can always expect people like Josh to be their own undoing."

"Oh come on!" said Miles. "You didn't know he'd order his own pantsing!"

"I didn't *know*," said Niles. "But I *hoped*."

Miles looked at Niles's face. The way he was smiling, it seemed like maybe he *had* been expecting this. Miles shook his head and turned back to the chaos below.

"Hey," said Niles. He was leaning forward now, his arms wrapped around his knees. "How'd you make those shine lines coming off Josh's underwear?"

"Oh," said Miles. "I ripped up one of my old T-shirts."

"What!" said Niles. "Which one?"

"My one from Max's Market."

"But—"

"It was getting ratty anyway."

Niles squinted in the fading light and admired the flag. "It looks cool. Like an Illuminati symbol or something."

"Yeah!" said Miles. "But with underwear!"

"Masterstroke," said Niles.

"Oh," said Miles.

Coming from Niles, that was a real compliment. And so Miles would remember their time on the hilltop his whole life too.

Soon enough, it was too dark to see, and the night was getting cold.

ONE LATE AUGUST MORNING, the air was suddenly cool. Sometimes autumn sneaks up early. On a rock near the swimming hole in the woods, the old gray goose lifted his beak to the air. He waggled his neck. He shook out his tail feathers. He waddled, then crouched, then spread out his wings. The goose pushed off the ground and launched himself into the air.

The goose flapped his wings but stayed low, for a goose. From fifty feet up, he got a good view of the woods. A grove, a lake, a little green glade. A cabin next to a big painted rock.

Down on the ground, a man in an olive green tracksuit looked up at the goose. Then he looked down and got back to reading the rock.

"Turn me over," he said. "Turn me over. But why?"

On all of his jogs through all parts of these woods, Tim had never seen a rock quite like this.

He scratched his square jaw.

It was probably someone's idea of a joke.

On the other hand, what was under that rock???????

He set both hands on the rock and pushed.

It was too heavy to move.

This was idiotic.

It was dumb.

And his heart rate was falling out of the cardio zone.

He continued his jog.

Still, what was under that rock???????

He'd come back this afternoon and bring a camper to help. Josh Barkin maybe. He was strong. He could lift things. And he could use a morale boost after that incident with the flag. It was the last day of camp. Josh could end on a high note. He and Josh could bond and turn over that rock.

The goose came out of the woods and flew over the town. Outside an ice cream shop, three kids stood on the sidewalk holding waffle cones.

Holly ran her hand across Niles's hair.

"Feels cool," Holly said. "Looks good too. You needed a haircut."

"What?" Niles asked.

"True," said Miles.

"*What?*" Niles asked.

A kid in a Hawaiian shirt ran across the street. "G'DAY, guys! That means HELLO! In AUSTRAL—what the WHAT the WHAT!"

"Hi, Stuart," said Niles.

"You CHANGED your LOOK!"

"Yeah," Niles said.

"Your OLD hair was BETTER!"

The goose passed over the town, over pastures and cows, over a squat brick building.

(It was a school.)

There was only one car in a huge parking lot, a yellow hatchback parked in the principal's spot.

Principal Barkin was arranging letters on the marquee.

"School, school, school," he sang to himself, "next week it's school."

He liked to get back to school early and make sure everything was shipshape: that the gym floor was waxed and the janitor's closet stocked. He went in each classroom and sharpened some pencils, so the smell of fresh cedar shavings would greet teachers and students. And last but not least—certainly not least!—he picked out a welcome message for the marquee.

Principal Barkin had come up with several good options:

"PRINCIPAL BARKIN SEZ: BACK TO SCHOOL! BACK TO COOL!"

"PRINCIPAL BARKIN SEZ: FALL BACK INTO LEARNING!"

"PRINCIPAL BARKIN SEZ: YAWNEE VALLEY *SCIENCE* AND *LETTERS* AND *FUN* ACADEMY!"

He liked that last one a lot, but the letters for the marquee didn't have italics, and he was afraid the students would miss the point.

But then he came up with something. The best message yet. Which just goes to show, if you keep going past good, you'll end up with great. He scrambled the letters till the marquee said:

YAWNEE VALLEY SCIENCE AND LETTERS ACADEMY

PRINCIPAL BARKIN SEZ:

WELCOME BACK, BOVINES!

LET'S MAKE THIS OUR BEST YEAR!!!

Principal Barkin admired his work.

Higher now, more than a mile over the ground, the gray goose joined fifteen other gray geese. He honked. They honked back. This was his flock. He loved his time at the swimming hole, alone, in the woods. And he loved rejoining his flock, when they all beat their wings, and flew high, and flew south. They were flying toward summer, the summer ahead. Behind them, in Yawnee Valley, the summer was done.

ABOUT *the* AUTHORS

MAC BARNETT is the *New York Times* bestselling author of more than 30 books for children, including the Brixton Brothers mystery series and the picture books *Extra Yarn*, and *Sam & Dave Dig a Hole*, both illustrated by Jon Klassen and both winners of a Caldecott Honor and the E. B. White Read-Aloud Award. He lives in Oakland, California.

JORY JOHN is a *New York Times* bestselling author of books for both children and adults. He is a two-time E.B. White Read-Aloud Honor recipient. Jory's work includes the picture books *Penguin Problems*, illustrated by Lane Smith, *Goodnight Already!*, illustrated by Benji Davies, and *The Bad Seed*, illustrated by Pete Oswald. He also co-authored numerous humor books, including the internationally bestselling *All My Friends Are Dead*. He spent six years as programs director at 826 Valencia, a nonprofit educational center in San Francisco. He resides in Oregon.

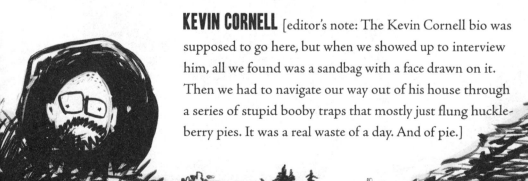

KEVIN CORNELL [editor's note: The Kevin Cornell bio was supposed to go here, but when we showed up to interview him, all we found was a sandbag with a face drawn on it. Then we had to navigate our way out of his house through a series of stupid booby traps that mostly just flung huckleberry pies. It was a real waste of a day. And of pie.]

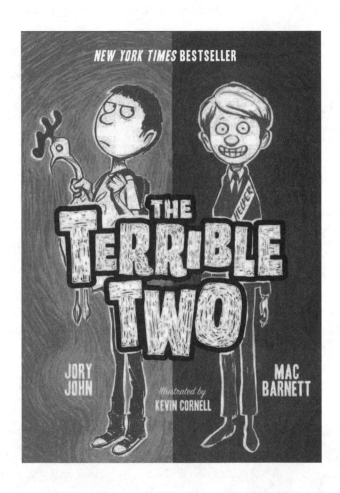

FOR SUSAN

Cataloging-in-Publication Data has been applied for and may be obtained from the Library of Congress.
ISBN 978-1-4197-2185-4

ISBN for this edition:
978-1-4197-2341-4

Text copyright © 2018 Mac Barnett and Jory John
Illustrations copyright © 2018 Kevin Cornell
Book design by Chad W. Beckerman

Printed and bound in U.S.A.
10 9 8 7 6 5 4 3 2 1

Amulet Books are available at special discounts when purchased in quantity for premiums and promotions as well as fundraising or educational use. Special editions can also be created to specification. For details, contact specialsales@abramsbooks.com or the address below.

ABRAMS The Art of Books
161 Farringdon Road, London EC1R 3AL
abramsandchronicle.co.uk